DOVE SEASON

ROBIN BRANDE

RYER PUBLISHING

DOVE SEASON
(Dove Season)
By Robin Brande

Published by Ryer Publishing
www.ryerpublishing.com
Copyright 2025 by Robin Brande
www.robinbrande.com
"The Canyon" was published in *Pulphouse* Magazine Issue #33
www.pulphousemagazine.com
Cover art by HoryMa/Deposit Photos
Cover design by Ryer Publishing
All rights reserved.
Print ISBN: 978-1-952383-25-0
Ebook ISBN: 978-1-946627-97-1

~

ALSO BY ROBIN BRANDE

<u>Dove Season Universe</u>

Dove Season

Finder

Seeker

Believer

Maker

Explorer

<u>Winnie Parsons Mysteries</u>

A Mind for Mysteries

The Genius Track

A Man of Appetites

A Drop of Sweat

The Long Gray Hook

The Slip of a Rib

The Cabin Ghost

The Secret Juror

<u>Parallelogram Quartet</u>

Into the Parallel

Caught in the Parallel

Seize the Parallel

Beyond the Parallel

Young Adult

Evolution, Me & Other Freaks of Nature

Fat Cat

Doggirl

Replay

Bradamante Saga

Book of Earth

Book of Water

Romance

Love Proof

Freefall

Heart of Ice

Fire and Ice

Collections

The Love of a Good Dog

Mountain Tough

The Miraculous Unknown

Self-Help

What If You're Doing It Right?

What If You're Doing It Right? For Teens

CONTENTS

DOVE SEASON UNIVERSE
RECOMMENDED READING ORDER

Dove Season

Finder

Seeker

Believer

Maker

Explorer

DOVE SEASON

DOVE SEASON

I can only work places that allow a smoke break. I don't smoke. My problem is different from that. My problem looks magical to other people, but it's a compulsion, something I can't resist, the way some people need coffee at the exact same times every day, or a sugar fix, or drugs, I suppose, although that's taking it further than I like.

I fly.

Specifically: I walk quickly for a few steps, then I bound forward a few steps more, and then I leap and I flap my arms (I am not joking) and by now I'm airborne and I can hover there, but I prefer to swim. I like doing butterfly. I arc both arms at the same time, wide big arms, feels beautiful and graceful and strong to do it that way, and I kick my feet together behind me in the dolphin kick I learned on swim team when I was little (before I could fly), and my body sort of undulates, although that sounds awful when I say it that way, but it's that kind of writhing forward thing a snail does, front end forward, big arm stroke, head dips down, butt comes up, here's the dolphin kick. I can cover acres of ground like that. I once air-swam from one end of a three-mile park to another all during my ten-minute smoke break.

I know, it sounds awesome. You wish you were me. I get it.

I used to have flying dreams. We all have, right? Where you're being chased by the bad guys and suddenly you realize if you run just a little faster and flap your arms, oh my gawd, you're lifting up, you're just out of their reach, you've escaped, you're safe, and now you might as well keep flying and seeing what that's like before you wake up—

Except all of that happened to me and I didn't wake up. Turns out this was my life now.

All fine, all good, except for the compulsion part. Remember I said about that? Because it turns out something like this isn't really as voluntary as you'd think. You can do it whenever you want, sure, but you also *have* to do it. If you don't, you feel sick and edgy and jittery and weak. You feel nauseous. You feel like you're going to jump out of your skin if you can't break away right now and do your walking-running-flying bit, and as soon as you do, as soon as you're airborne again, it's like all the jittery, frayed endings of your nerves have been knit back together and fixed. It is a fix. I admit it. And I need it every single hour.

So no. No thank you. I refuse. Can I go now?

Because my hour was long past—*long* past. Did they not get that? Did they want to see what would happen? Of course they did. Tricky government men with their tough-guy too-tight short-sleeved buttoned-down shirts like they don't know they should go up a size and stop strutting around their gymmed-up pecs like a woman wearing a small when she's a 36. Come on. Boring. I've seen it.

I told them as little as possible, but I know I said too much. As the time ticked by I was becoming more desperate, and you say things. They count on that.

But then the door opened, someone new coming in, and quick as a lark I was up and out of my chair, out the door, running, running, desperate for open air.

"Miss Stemple? Marnie?" He was running after me, the shorter, younger one with the tight blue shirt, sweat stains in his pits, crooked front teeth but good thick brown hair, not a bad face overall, but still. Effen government men. They'd had me in there for over three—THREE—hours, studying me, questioning me, thinking they were convincing me ("Service to your country … make a huge difference … fulfill your purpose. Don't you *want* to fulfill your purpose, Miss Stemple?")

F you, I made a mistake, that short-necked guy from accounts payable with the Hitler-looking comb-over saw me, friggin *saw* me, and if he thinks this is serving his country by calling the feds and telling them he saw a flier, some woman right there from his own office, then F you all, and THREE HOURS, my heart was racing, cold clammy sweat was pouring down my face, my heart was going 500, my eyes were already scanning out the windows for where I could go, someplace tall where I could fly, but there was nothing, no place, not even a few trees on the medians, and still I ran full out.

"Marnie!" I could hear the gym guy's flat government feet pounding hard against the fake tile floor, but I was running faster than he was, faster than anyone ever can, because I can do that (run, run, flap), it's my *life*, and the hour, you idiots, did you think I was lying about how it feels? Exaggerating? You think it's funny? Something I can turn off?

Burst out the doors, everyone looking, but I couldn't help it, I was dying, I was crying and dying, then finally *run, run, flap, flap again*, and gawwwwd. Oh gawd. The air the freedom the lift the pleasure the release the relief the HEAVEN.

But crying. Sobbing. So relieved and happy and anguished.

Butterfly. My beautiful butterfly stroke. And all those people down below shielding their eyes with their flattened palms, staring up at me so amazed, some of them applauding. F you! Don't you understand what you've done?

Because now I have to leave again. Leave immediately. Can I even go home first? Pack a light pack? Get it slung over my back and get airborne again before the feds show up and surround me?

What would they do? Bring a net? Shoot me? Tranq me?

Still crying, snot running down my chin, but the air

swishes it away. The air beautiful air. If I say it's like a lover it sounds like I love this. Like I want this. I don't. I want what everyone has.

"How long have you had this power?"

"It's not a power."

"Of course it is, Miss Stemple."

"Then a gift," said the other one, the older one with the tight tan shirt. *"Call it a gift."*

"It's not a gift, it's not a power, can I go now? Can you legally hold me? This is America. You can't hold me." (Checked my watch, even though I didn't need a watch to tell me it was past an hour. Way past an hour. Feet tapping the floor. Jittery. Nerves thrumming. Come on, come on, I have to go. If someone had to pee now would you make them sit here and wet themselves? Can you do that to someone who's not under arrest? Am I under arrest? This is physical. It's real. I've gotta *go*—)

Two minutes in the beautiful air. That's all it ever takes. I could already feel my heart beating normally again, loving me again, all of the pasty clammy sweat dried off my skin.

They were in their government cars. Had to be. They knew my address. They were already driving to my apartment, I knew it.

All that furniture I bought over the past six months. Thinking I could stay. Thinking because the office was right across from the park, all those lovely dark tall trees, I could hide it better this time. Get into the trees and just flap straight up. No big deal. Just a quickie, then right back to work.

But that flippin stalker with the Hitler haircut—did he follow me? On purpose? Or was it just his luck to see me step, step, leap, flap, straight from the ground to the boughs ten feet up?

Did he rush back and call right then? Did he take *pictures?* The feds never showed me pictures, but they were awfully confident if it was just someone calling on a tip line. Had to be more. I've gotten sloppy. I'm only twenty-eight. Too young to be so lazy.

Go *where?*

Maybe back to Pinedale, Wyoming. No one ever saw me there. I was Marjorie Dunham there. Strictly cash, my ex-husband is still looking for me (no ex-husband, lie), let's not use my social security number, he might find me.

Marjorie wore corduroys and sweaters and knit hats and comfy boots. She had a cat, some stray that showed up one day and stayed. Marjorie had friends. Not many, but even one feels like a dream. Marjorie had plenty of trees, glorious trees, right there outside her little rented house in the woods and right outside the insurance office where she kept books. Marjorie was happy there. Until she wasn't.

Then how about Millie? Millie drove an old beater truck and lived in Clinton, Iowa and even dated a few times before realizing that would *never* work, someone noticing you leave every hour, even in the middle of the night? Ha ha, I'm a vampire. No, seriously, I just love the night air. Come back to bed... No, *seriously*, I have to leave...

By now I could see my apartment building. Corner

unit, bottom floor, because it's no help to live up high on a top floor, I still always need those few steps and the leap before I can flap.

No obviously government cars. What would they drive? Black sedans? White? Would all the cars look the same, four or five of them all in a row? I couldn't see anything like that.

I came down my usual way into the trees half a block away, then jogged toward my building, heart racing again as I scanned the streets looking for suspicious people and cars. It was a risk, I knew it. For what? A few favorite items of clothing? A wad of money hidden in my closet? No cat this time, no friends to say goodbye to, so why was I even bothering? But I was and I was at my door now and I quickly unlocked it and ducked inside.

Then I stood there, back against my door. Looked around. What was my life? That couch, the laptop (scooped that up, not too heavy to weigh me down), no photos, no mementos, my favorite sleep shirt—stuff that in the pack, too—a comfortable pair of shoes, underwear, sweats, that's enough, you have to go, Marnie, *go*—

Bam bam bam!

"Miss Stemple?" *Bam bam bam.* "Marnie? Please let me in. It's just me. Ted. I'm alone. Please, let's talk."

Ted. The one with the crooked teeth and the thick brown hair.

Other places I've lived had back doors. Not this one. Windows? Yes, but not feasible. Small and hard to open. Dammit dammit *dammit.*

Knock, knock, knock. Politely. "Please, Miss Stemple. I want to make you an offer."

I ran away from these guys once, I could run again. But not now. There was no way now.

I was full up again on flying. Enough to last me at least another hour, maybe even a little bit longer.

But you can't trust a government man. Well known.

But I was trapped.

I looked out through the peephole. I only saw him. My heart was speeding. My skin felt clammy again. But it was only fear, not the compulsion, so I could deal with it. I took a deep breath and unlocked the door.

He really was alone. And the pit stains on his tight blue shirt were even bigger, as if he had run all that way while I flew. He smelled a little worse than he did even in that cooped up tiny room. But not so bad I didn't let him in.

We stood there on the little patch of linoleum right inside my door before where the matted brown carpet began and we took the measure of each other.

"I know you don't want this—" he started.

"I don't."

"I know you don't trust us."

"I don't."

He held up his palms. "No weapons." He patted his tight shirt. "No wire." He patted down his pockets and lifted his pant hems and showed me he wasn't wearing or carrying anything that I might object to.

"It's just me," he said. "But please, I have to know. I have to understand. Just you and me. Will you tell me?"

I took a step back, onto the safety of the dark brown carpet. "Tell you what?"

"Why?" he said. "Why you really don't want to do something with this wonderful gift of yours?"

"Because if *you* had it…"

"Right," said Ted. "That's what I'm thinking."

"That's what *everyone* would think."

"Tell you the truth," Ted said, "I'm about dying here. I could really use a glass of water, if you don't mind. But then I've got all day. And all night, and tomorrow and next week."

"You think you're just staying here until I talk?"

"I'm *asking* you," Ted said. "I swear I'll respect you if you still tell me no, but I'm a psychologist at heart and I can't just let you leave without trying to understand why."

"Who says I'm leaving?"

He tilted his head as if to say, *Right.*

So I got him the water.

Then I let him sit on my six-month-old couch that I bought thinking it might last me a full year.

I perched on my desk chair. Swiveled it a few times while I worked up my nerve. No weapons, no wire, just him. Just a guy. Some government psychology guy who wanted to know how I think. Or how I feel. Same thing, all part of the same story.

Just this once. Tell someone the story just once. Some kind of compulsion of its own.

"When I was nineteen," I began, still not sure, "I saw an article in a magazine about a place called Willcox, Arizona. It looked so remote and pretty, with all these beautiful rock formations I'd never seen anyplace else. The rocks were huge and round like giant balls of dough. They weren't jagged like you see anyplace else. And there was so much land. Miles and miles of it. And apple trees —lots of orchards and apple tree farms. I thought it would be a nice place to live."

Ted sipped his water. I took another breath. Should I tell him this story? Should I tell anyone?

"I got there in late September, and the weather was perfect. I'd been living in the mountains for the first part of the year, and I knew the winter would be hard, so I wanted someplace milder, just until spring. Then I'd look for someplace else."

"Is that what you've been doing?" Ted asked. "Moving around every few months?"

"Sometimes," I said. "If I can stay longer, I do."

"What's your longest?"

"Almost two years."

Ted nodded. "Go on."

He wasn't taking notes. This wasn't an interview. He was just listening.

"I found a job. I won't say what. Don't bother looking, it was under a different name."

"Do you do that, too? Every time?"

"I'm… not going to say." He was a government man. I've been careful. Cash only, no records. That wasn't part of the story.

"I was there September, October, November. Until Thanksgiving. I liked it. I liked the people. I liked how barren a lot of it was. I always need trees, but I could still visit all that wide open space and the rounded rocks and there were canyons and streams and it was all like a book. It was the Wild West. It was a beautiful place to fly."

"Did something happen there?" Ted asked. He probably couldn't help himself, his psychology training kicking in. It irritated me, because suddenly it didn't feel like a natural conversation anymore, more like a session of some sort. But I let it go.

To a degree.

"What will you do with this information?" I asked.

"Nothing."

"You'll have to report it, right?"

"Not necessarily."

I scoffed. "You work for people. You don't get to just come ask me questions and then never tell anyone."

"We'll see," said Ted. "You don't have to tell me any more if you don't want. But I'd really love to hear."

I bit the inside of my lip. Glanced up at the clock. It had been almost forty minutes, between deciding whether to let him in, letting him in, getting him water, deciding whether to tell, and telling that much so far.

"I have to go soon," I said. "You know."

Ted nodded. "Go on. Thanksgiving."

"Thanksgiving was nice. The diner did a whole spread. I took a plate home. I hadn't eaten that well in a while. The people in the diner seemed happy. I really liked the waitress who was working. She was older, probably my mother's age, and she was always so nice to me."

If he were really interviewing me, he would have perked up at some of that: *"Which diner? What was the waitress's name? How old is your mother? What's her name?"* But he just kept listening.

"But it was the day after," I said. "That was the thing.

"I flew out right at dawn, the way I always love to. Out over all those wide open spaces.

"I heard gunfire. Lots of it.

"Up ahead, over the grain fields, I saw shapes of things falling out of the sky. *Bam!* Something fall. *Bam bam!* Something fall. I landed a ways away because it wasn't safe to be in the air right then, and I ran to where it was happening to see what it was.

"It was dove season. I didn't know. Hunters and their dogs all combing the grain fields and shooting at all the birds who had come there to eat.

"Dozens and dozens and probably fifty or more dead by the time they were done. Just a few hours right after dawn and all these men and women shooting at those poor innocent birds.

"I'm telling you," I said, tears stinging my eyes, "I was *broken*. Something broke in me. All those pretty, innocent birds.

"No, but here's the thing," I said, swiping beneath my eyes, "it wasn't just that. It probably would have been, but then it got worse. At dusk, they all came back."

"The hunters."

"The *birds*. Even though they'd been shot at already and so many of them were killed, the flocks still came back to that same grain field for dinner. And the same hunters, or maybe all new ones, didn't matter, *blam, blam,* little gray bodies twisting in the air, feathers exploding with the shot, dogs racing out and chasing down some of the birds who were still trying to flap on the ground with still one good wing, and the dogs chomped down on them and then carried them back so proud to their owners…

"And I know the birds would have come back the next morning. And the next night. And do it day after day until dove season ended, dying and not able to help themselves, because they just *had* to do it."

I stopped talking. It was enough. If he got it, he got it. If he didn't, he couldn't.

Ted seemed comfortable with the silence. He leaned back on my couch and stared at some speck on my rented ceiling. Minutes ticked by. I had to fly soon.

Finally he asked, "What is your concern?"

"My concern?"

He looked me in the eye. "Yes."

I blew out a breath. (*"Don't you want to serve your country, Miss Stemple? Don't you want to fulfill your purpose?"*)

"Look at me," I said, gesturing down to my bird-thin body and scrawny arms and wispy legs. "I'm not tough. I can't fight. I don't know martial arts. I hate guns. I hate violence of any kind."

Ted listened. And waited.

"You can't send me up there," I said. "Not for some military mission. Not for some… secret government work. I'm defenseless. I'm useless. Yes, I can fly. But that's all. Nothing else. I'd be dead the first day."

Ted nodded. "I understand."

"I have to go," I said hurriedly. "Can I go?"

"Of course." He stood politely. But he didn't move toward the door.

I hesitated. Should I wait? See him out? Lock the door before flapping away?

He seemed to understand my discomfort. "How long?"

"I can… just ten minutes."

"I'll wait if it's all right."

The buzz was inside me. I had to go. *Fly, fly now.*

"Don't look at anything, don't snoop—"

He held up his palms and sat back down on my couch. "Maybe another glass of water, but nothing else. I promise."

I opened the door and ran out. It wouldn't matter if he snooped anyway. I'm used to leaving everything behind. There's nothing for anyone to see.

I ran to my favorite tree, skip, leap, flap, and I was up there before anyone could see me. Just a taste of it, a ten-minute smoke-break taste. Enough. I needed to get back.

He was still sitting on the couch, but he was right, he was drinking more water. I got some water, too. Flying is dehydrating.

"And if someone caught me," I went on as if there had been no break. "You saw how I was today. If someone tried to keep me locked up…"

"If we could address your concerns," Ted said. "All of them." He stopped there and waited, as if that were enough.

My mouth felt dry. I tried to swallow just the same.

But my voice sounded croaky and weak. "I can't help myself," I said. "Just like the doves. I'd know it was dangerous, but I wouldn't be able to stop."

Ted stood. He offered me his hand. The flesh was warm and dry. The pit stains on his shirt were dry now, too. He smelled like he had worked a full day. I didn't mind it so much.

"Please don't leave," he said. "I know you want to, but just give me a day or two."

"Until what?"

"We know people," he said. "We can do things. We can make things. I understand your concerns. I really do, Marnie. Is that your real name?"

I hesitated, then nodded.

"We won't try to make you do anything. That doesn't work. We know that."

He was back to sounding like a government man. *We we we...*

He handed me his card. *Ted Whitling.* Just his name and a phone number. No address, no email, nothing else. If I had met him anywhere else and he had handed me that card, I would have thrown it in the trash. You have to let people look you up these days. People need to be able to do their research.

But I already knew he worked in a two-story gray brick building with a flat roof and no trees nearby, and he had a security pass that let him in and out of a tiny windowless room where they interrogate prisoners like me who haven't done anything wrong. That was his job.

Here he was in my tidy rented living room, but he belonged back there where everyone in the building from the agents to the janitors knew I was a flier and had watched me do it.

If I stuck around, how was I any smarter than a dove flying back to the grain field?

"Marnie?"

Fifty more minutes, and I'd fly again. Just fifty more minutes.

The question was, fly how? Fly where? Just a ten-minute flap up into some trees and a few glorious strokes of butterfly, or flying for distance and speed with a light pack on my back, searching for my next life to lead?

"We can do things," he repeated. "Just wait for me. Please."

It was the *please.*

"Sure you don't want to eat here, honey? Everyone needs people around them for the holidays. You're gonna just take a plate home? Sure I can't get you more pie?"

"Yes, please," I told the motherly waitress. *"That would be nice."*

"I love a young lady who says 'please,'" she said. *"We're a world without manners. You just wait right there ten more minutes. Fresh pie is almost out of the oven."*

But I didn't have ten minutes. I barely had five. I had to grab my food and drive off so I could get in my afternoon flight. Even on Thanksgiving. A compulsion is a compulsion. The holidays don't change that.

"Can you get rid of it?" I suddenly thought to ask Ted.

It had never occurred to me that it might be possible. *We can do things*. Do this.

"I would never want to get rid of it," he said. "I hope I can make you feel the same way."

He gave me a polite nod and stepped toward my door. He was about to open it when he turned to me.

"I do understand," he said. "About the doves. About you flying around out there and seeing that. It must have been terrible."

Maybe it was just a psychology trick, but it seemed like he meant it. I swallowed dry air and nodded.

"But maybe we can find a way for you to be safe and not just have to fly ten minutes at a time," he said. "Maybe you can fly anytime you want, for as long as you want. If we can give you that, will you take it?"

I stared at him, wide-eyed and alarmed. *Here's a warehouse full of your favorite drug, junkie. Here's all the nicotine in the world. Here's a bottomless barrel of booze. Fly all you want. You never have to stop. We can make it your job to fly...*

"Two days," Ted said. "Can you wait for me two days?"

My heart was speeding again. Dammit, my heart was yearning.

What if we could protect the flock feeding in the grain fields? What if the hunters had no guns? What if the doves wore protective flight suits? What if what if what if?

"I don't know," I said. "I have to think about it." Forty-three more minutes to flight.

"There are thousands of people with gifts and powers of their own," Ted said. "But you don't know about them, do you?"

"No," I had to admit.

"We're very good at keeping secrets. We're very good at helping people use their talents. Let us help you, Marnie." He shook my hand again. I'm sure he could feel me trembling. No better than a junkie. But if there really were some way…

Fly any time I want. Fly as long as I want. Fly protected. Fly forever.

"You'd probably make up some name for me," I said sarcastically, trying to sound both tough and brave. I could already feel my resolve fading. I was losing my edge. I was stepping into danger. I knew it but I couldn't help myself.

"We generally let people name themselves," he said.

The Dove, I thought automatically. That would capture both the stupidity and the compulsion of it. Maybe I'd wait the two days. It was just two days. But in two days he *had* to convince me. I didn't see how he could do it.

"Let me get to work," said Ted. "I won't disappoint you."

He left and closed the door. Thirty-eight more minutes until I needed my fix.

What if I could go any time I wanted? Would I ever stop flying? When would I eat? When would I sleep? When do the doves sleep? Heads tucked under their wings on some branch? That didn't sound bad. Just a quick nap on my couch, then back up in the air.

I exhaled a long, slow breath. Danger, and already I was getting used to it. I started packing a light pack anyway, just in case. My laptop, my sleep shirt, the comfy shoes.

You can't trust the feds. Well known.

But I'm a flier. No one can catch me once I fly.

The doves probably think that, too.

Thirty-six more minutes.

Heaven help me, I have to fly.

ANALYST

1

"I have a rule," Gina said as she steered me bodily down the aisles. It was a little past nine in the morning and the bookstore had barely opened.

I had just shot a man six hours earlier. I still felt shaky, even though the killing was necessary.

Analysts don't usually kill. We sit and read all day and think. But sometimes your theories bear out before you're ready to be right, and I was too right too fast.

I hiked up the waist on the workout pants Gina had lent me. They'd whisked me out of my apartment so fast I didn't have time to grab clothes of my own. My pajamas were still splattered with blood. I wore one of Gina's shirts too, a couple of sizes too big. Built like an Amazon, she had at least six inches on me. I got my height from my petite Filipino mother instead of my tall German-American father.

I continued to let Gina lead me. I didn't want to be

there. I needed sleep and solitude and time to think, but Gina and her fellow investigators had been at me for hours. *"Who did you tell about your research? Who else in the department knew? Walk us through the steps. How did you find out about Danic?"*

But the real question was how did Danic find out about *me*? We had a traitor in our midst and we knew it. We all felt duly unnerved.

"Did you know it was him when you shot him?"

"No, not until I turned on the light."

His eyes were open, mouth slightly agape, as if he'd died surprised. I kicked away his lethal-looking knife and automatically checked for a pulse. I didn't want to touch him, but the training kicked in.

I recognized him. The shaggy blond hair thinning on top, the particular slope of his nose. I'd seen him in some of the surveillance photos I'd been studying for the past week. He wasn't even my primary target. He kept showing up in groups of men I meant to investigate separately as soon as I'd mapped out my broader theory.

If I hadn't already seen his face so many times I would have thought he was just a random thug breaking in.

He hadn't expected an alarm to go off. Not in some low-rent studio apartment. Then it was a matter of his reflexes versus mine. If I'd been slower, groggier, I'd be the one dead right now. Stabbed with that sharp ugly blade that clattered from his hand when my bullet met his chest in the dark.

I dialed the Agency's emergency number and they told

me to wait, don't touch anything. I stood in my small clean kitchen and couldn't take my eyes off the body.

Danic was solid and beefy. He wore cheap-looking black polyester pants, black sneakers, and a black cotton zip-up jacket. Blood was already spreading out from beneath him onto my fake wood floor. I went back and jerked away the nearby rug before the blood could reach it.

I could still smell his blood, even now, hours later. The stench of it seemed stuck to the inside of my nostrils. Gina was supposed to be taking me to a hotel where I could finally shower and get some sleep. But she'd insisted on this detour first.

"Here," she said, finally coming to a stop in front of a row of bookshelves.

Comic books.

I'm sure I looked at her with disgust. This wasn't funny. This wasn't okay. Maybe she killed people every week, but I wasn't in the habit.

She was a senior agent, but I didn't care about rank. I turned and started walking away.

"Alice—" She grabbed my arm and twisted me around.

I saw movement directly behind her.

"React," my uncles always told me. *"Don't think, react."*

You do drills over and over to get your reflexes tuned so you fight before you know why you're fighting.

Gina made a sound and I pushed her hard to my left and leapt past her to the man wearing glasses. He hadn't been there ten seconds before. The knife in his hand was wet and red with blood that I knew must be Gina's.

He stabbed toward my chest.

I angled my body away from the blade and slammed my palm into his wrist. His meaty fist still held fast to the handle.

"Fight once. Finish the fight. Don't keep fighting the same person twice."

He slashed toward my rib and I warded again and this time I stomped hard sideways against his knee. He grunted as his right leg gave way, and he tried to stab me again.

But he was at my own height now, with his throat perfectly poised, and it doesn't take strength to crush a man's windpipe. You have to be fast, and I am, my uncles made sure of it, and they always taught me to aim.

Maybe the Agency would want him alive to find out whatever he knew, but he was a man with a knife and he was trying to kill me. I punched my fist hard into his throat. His body fell backward to the ground and I was glad.

Gina gasped. Gasped again. She was struggling to breathe.

I dropped down beside her. Blood leaked from a wound in her back. From the sound of her breathing, the attacker had pierced her lung. I pressed my hand firmly against the wound.

Three bookstore clerks stood nearby, frozen in place and staring.

"Call an ambulance," I told them. "Right now." I saw one of the girls pull out her phone. "And bring me some towels," I told the other two. I needed a better way to staunch the blood.

The man with the knife still hadn't moved. I wasn't surprised he was dead. It didn't bother me the way killing Danic had. Doing it with my hands instead of a gun felt more natural. I had been practicing that since I was six.

Gina gasped again and clutched hard at my arm. Her eyes looked wide and desperate. Her lips were starting to turn blue.

"They're coming," I told her, and kept pressing on the wound. There was nothing else I could do.

2

It took a while to sort it all out. Gina in one ambulance, sirens blaring, the dead man in another, sirens silent. Me back to the Agency for another barrage of questions.

But finally someone showed up with a bag of fresh clothes from my apartment, and one of Gina's colleagues drove me to a hotel.

I took a long hot shower. I ate a burger and salad from room service. I drank a carafe of stale coffee and then I slept hard for the next seven hours.

I woke to a message on my phone: Gina was alive. She wanted to see me.

I smiled and my throat felt tight and tears misted my eyes. I hadn't been sure she would make it. People die. I had spent the last few years since my parents died forcing myself to get used to it.

It was why I joined the Agency. Why I looked into files of men like Danic.

I changed into jeans and sneakers and a black T-shirt. Then I dialed the number of my new personal guard. No more wandering freely on my own. My escort, a six-foot-three solid-looking agent named Santos, drove me to the hospital.

I found Gina's room on the east wing of the third floor and pushed the door to go inside.

Her face still looked fairly gray. But her eyes were open and she was talking.

An agent I didn't know was standing beside her, taking notes on a yellow pad. He was mid-30s, I guessed, stocky and athletic-looking, with brown hair cut short to his scalp.

I thought I had seen him around the Agency before, but I couldn't be sure. Two nurses were in the room too, adjusting tubes and checking monitors. Gina looked past them all and smiled when she saw it was me.

She held up a finger for me to wait. Then she said something to the man with the notepad. He turned around and looked at me and gave me a brief but serious nod. He and Gina spoke in low tones for another minute more, then he thanked her and turned to go.

He paused in front of me and held out his hand.

"Ted Whitling."

"Alice Kern."

"We'll be speaking, Alice," he said, then he continued on to the door.

Gina reached out her right arm and drew me into a

half hug. Her left side was heavily bandaged. I could see the bulk of it under her hospital gown.

"How are you feeling?" I asked.

"Hurts like hell," she said. "Here, grab a chair. Sit close, I want to talk."

She waited for the nurses to leave.

"That wasn't on your application," she said.

I knew what she meant. I had been thinking about it since the attack. Expecting someone to bring it up.

We're supposed to list any relevant training we've had: weapons, boxing, combat… martial arts.

I left that section blank. On purpose.

I never mentioned it in any interviews. In fact, when the recruiters and anyone else ever asked me, I outright lied.

I wanted to be an analyst. Not a field agent. I wanted access to the Agency's records. I wanted to find the truth.

Other people could fight the bad guys. I wanted to be the one who found them. All of them. Starting with the ones who had taken my parents from me.

"No," I told Gina, "it wasn't."

"I assume you had a reason."

I nodded.

"I appreciate you saving my life."

I nodded again. I wasn't really sure what to say. What was going to happen to me now? I assumed Gina had to include it in her report. Maybe that's what that Ted guy meant. *"We'll be speaking, Alice."* Maybe he was in charge of reassigning people.

Would I have any say in it? Or would there be a transfer order waiting for me back at the office?

"I don't want to go in the field," I told Gina. "I want to stay an analyst."

"You can handle yourself," she said. "Obviously. Two attacks the same day, two attackers dead."

"I want to know *why*," I said. "I don't even know who the second guy was. I don't remember him from any of my files."

"You're going to have to leave that to us for a while," she said. It was exactly what I was afraid of.

"So they're taking me off it?"

"It's just temporary," she said. "You need to get out of town for a while. We'd be stupid to keep you here. We assume you were the target in the bookstore, not me." She gestured toward her bandages. "I think I was just in his way."

I let out a sigh. It wasn't what I wanted, but it was going to be hard to argue they were wrong. Danic knew where I lived. The man with glasses had followed us to the bookstore. There was a reason monolithic-looking Santos was standing outside Gina's hospital room door right now wearing a gun and at least two knives.

"I think you'll like your next posting," said Gina. She cracked a slight smile. "Which finally gets me back to my rule."

She pointed to the nearby bedside table that had been shifted out of the way by one of the nurses. "I had one of my pals go get those. Treat them carefully—they're my only copies."

I got up and walked over to the table. There were four or five comic books on top of it. What was it with the comics? Gina seemed too serious to be the type.

"I've been in this job ten years," she said. "It took me at least half of that to figure this out. I'm going to try to save you the trouble." She shrugged. "You can believe me or not.

"I used to work this job all hours," she went on, "just like I'm sure you do. There's always so much more to read, right? So much new material you have to get through."

She was right, of course. I was less than a year on the job, greener than green, and so far every day the work seemed to multiply. I was working seven days a week, fourteen hours in the office, more hours once I got home. I kept feeling further and further behind. I didn't have enough eyeballs or brain cells to master all the new information flooding in to me every day in stacks of paper or files on my screen.

"Do you ever catch up?" I asked one of my co-workers one day.

"Never ever," Trey answered. "Ever. Ever, ever, ever, ever, infinity."

And it wasn't just the assigned work. It was also the project I was pursuing on my own. That's what I worked on at night. I resented having to sleep.

"You can't keep it up," said Gina. "It's not physically or mentally possible. You probably think you're different, but I thought that too. You'll burn out. You'll lose it. And then you're no good to any of us." She paused and looked me squarely in the eye. "Alice, are you listening to me?"

I nodded. But it didn't really apply. I was only twenty-six. I wasn't close to burning out.

"I have a rule that at night," Gina said, "I have to shut the work off. I can't look at anything on my computer. I can't read anything serious. No news, no nonfiction books, no depressing novels. Not even spy thrillers—they're too overstimulating.

"I read fantasy. Sword and sorcery. Books with magic. Comic books. Anything with clear-cut heroes and the good guys are guaranteed to win."

"That's great," I said, barely hiding my sarcasm, "but then at three in the morning some killer breaks into your apartment—"

"And you're fresh," Gina said. "Alert. Because you've been sleeping peacefully since ten o'clock."

I started to argue, to say there were never enough hours in the day, that it was great she could indulge herself like that, but I couldn't.

But Gina held up her hand to cut me off, and since she was the one with tubes going into her arm I let her.

"You're going to get a visit," Gina said. "Probably in the morning. You'll want to be dressed and prepped by eight. You're not coming back into the office. Not until we know it's safe."

I tried to hide my distress. They couldn't take me away from this—not yet, not if I was getting close. And the fact that two men had tried to kill me in the last twenty-four hours proved I was getting close.

"Ted Whitling," said Gina. "You just met him. He thinks he has a job for you."

"Doing what?" I asked suspiciously. I hadn't gotten a real feel for the man. Although based on how he looked, I had to assume he was in the field.

Gina pointed to the comics I now held in my hand. "Do your research. It's what you're good at. And then go where we need you to serve."

I looked down at the cover on top.

A snarling woman with long black hair and a blue chestplate held a sword at her side. She looked ferocious and deadly. Hiding behind her was a little child she appeared to be protecting.

I'll admit I was a little curious. I looked at the next cover in the stack. Same fierce warrior woman, same sword, but now incongruously a helicopter in the background.

"Just give them a try," said Gina. "Some light reading tonight. But trust me, you might actually find some parts of those useful."

"How?" I couldn't see how any of these related to real life.

I came to the last in the series. The warrior woman now had wings. They were huge, with alternating blue and black feathers. Outstretched, they took up almost all of the cover.

"Ted has a special case," Gina said. "He thinks you might be the right person to help."

She glanced at the clock on the wall behind me. It was

digital with oversized numbers. "I need to sleep," she told me. "You do too. You're going to be traveling for a while tomorrow. No more questions," she added, heading me off, "that's all I'm allowed to say."

She effectively kicked me out. Santos was waiting in the hall. I tried to hide the comics at my side, but I was sure he saw them and chose not to comment.

We stepped out of the hospital into the cool nighttime air. The digital clock on the wall had read 9:49. It seemed impossible that it was still the same day. Only nineteen hours had passed since Danic broke in and tried to stab me.

Back in the hotel I took another shower and changed into a clean T-shirt and sweats. I propped up the pillows on the king-sized bed and prepared to fire up my laptop.

Gina couldn't understand. This was just work to her. For me, it was my parents' lives.

They were both martial artists too. But that hadn't saved them in the end. As skilled as they were, they couldn't stop bullets. They couldn't defend themselves from a man they never saw. He shot them from too great a distance.

So yes, I too longed for a world where the good guys were guaranteed to win. But I wasn't a child. I wasn't naïve.

And I knew from everything I'd found so far that there was more to the shooting than anyone had been told.

But I was getting closer. Two dead men were proof of that.

I glanced again at Gina's collection of comics. The sword, the helicopter, the wings.

What work did the Agency have for me now?

I powered up my computer. I had more important work of my own.

FIVE STARS, THREE MOONS

1

Fritz Zimholt waited in the conservatory of the Bellagio hotel on an ivory-colored padded bench with his back to the lavish Christmas display. He rested his wooden cane against his leg. He didn't need it, but it was useful for the image he wanted to project.

Age seventy-four, white neatly-clipped beard, bald on top with white hair covering only the lower half of his scalp, he looked like any of the other old people around him who had lowered themselves exhausted onto chairs and benches, overwhelmed by the opulence, wearied by the crowd.

Fritz had no interest in the holiday display, but it had been hard to ignore. The giant toy soldiers revolving on pedestals made to look like toy drums. The polar bears cavorting on imitation chunks of ice in the fountain's pond. The oversized elves with their knife-thin noses, smiling next to their oversized ornaments. A vibrant carpet of poinsettias pretending to be a forest floor beneath an imitation Christmas tree as tall as the expansive arched ceiling. A bridge over the fountain, leading to a white fantasy castle. A team of four enormous white horses pulling a bubble-shaped white carriage to the imitation castle gate.

Fritz Zimholt hated all of it.

But the place was useful. Tourists from everywhere. Local Las Vegas families with their children. Grandparents indulging their wee ones, *Look at the horses! Look at the bears!*

Ingelene Blau came into view. Short, frumpy, as white-haired as Fritz, hair cut short the way old American women wore it, two grandchildren running ahead.

Fritz stood slowly. He was a hardy man, still capable of bench pressing what he did at sixty-five, still skiing in the Utah mountains, but for his purposes now he was frail, halting, dependent on the cane, needing to pause every few steps to catch his breath.

Ingelene was good. He knew she saw him, but of course she never let on.

At last he stood beside her, head tilted back, pretending to gaze up at the top of the ridiculous tree.

"Danic is dead," Ingelene said. "Killed by the Kern girl."

The news was unexpected, but not unwelcome.

"They're moving her," Ingelene continued. They could have spoken German to each other, but it might draw attention. Be memorable. The old German couple, he had a cane. Better to blend in, even though Ingelene still spoke with an accent. Sometimes these things were hard to lose.

Her grandchildren leaned over the railing to delight in the artificial polar bears. Ingelene smiled when the girl turned back, acknowledged the girl's "Look!" with a wave, never turned her head to look at Fritz.

"Where?"

"The Aviary," she said.

Also unexpected.

He wandered away. Pretended he was done admiring the tree and all its gaudy ornaments and the ugly, chunky stars hanging from the ceiling.

Ingelene wrapped her arms around her grandchildren and continued through the room to inspect more of the garish spectacle.

She would contact him when she learned more. Fritz had no doubt.

Walking with a limp, more slowly than his body liked, put tension on his knees and strained his back. He had learned not to hurry. When you are playing a part, you play it to the last. Even getting into a car, someone might have followed you, someone might notice if the old man suddenly stands upright, stretches his back, rolls his shoulders, slides easily onto his seat.

No, he would walk stooped all the way to the parking garage. Would be ginger as he took his place behind the steering wheel. Would drive leaning slightly forward, as if his eyesight wasn't good. He wore thick clear-lensed glasses for the same effect, even though his contacts served him well.

He had not been caught for the entire forty-seven years he had been doing this work.

He would not die in prison. He would not die at the end of a knife. Nor would the Kern girl. He would see to that.

2

Fritz climbed the stairs to the second floor of his house in the Wasatch mountains. Sunshine flooded the room. He had had the place built to take advantage of the sun. More, even, than the views of the hills.

"How was it?" his wife, Beverly, asked. She wore yoga pants and a loose-fitting pale blue top, and he could see her breasts when she leaned over to pick up his garment bag. She was fifty-one, still good looking for her age, with an ass that still held its shape.

Biking and hiking in the summers, skiing all winter long. The mountain lifestyle agreed with both of them. She had no lovers, Fritz was certain of it, and she seemed satisfied with what he could still do.

"It was good," he answered, kissing her and giving that ass a squeeze. They would make love later. It was their habit whenever he returned from a trip, even if he had been gone only a day.

His wife believed him when he said he was an executive with an oil company. She never questioned the hours he worked or the many trips he took. She seemed content with her life as an artist, hours spent sketching and painting the surrounding landscapes she could see even without ever stepping outside.

"What was the weather like?" Beverly asked. She set his luggage at the foot of the stairway up to the third-floor bedroom and returned to her work in the kitchen. She was hand mixing a thick batter in a bowl. She dipped her pinky in and licked it.

Fritz felt a slight arousal at that. "Windy," he said.

"But not snowing?"

He had been in Pittsburgh. That was what he said. Not sunny, dry Las Vegas.

"Not yet," Fritz answered. "Maybe by Christmas."

Utah had already been blanketed in it. He and Beverly had been skiing since a few days before Thanksgiving. Fritz loved the snow, but regretted the gray skies that came with it. He preferred the spring when snow was thick and established, and almost every day was sunny.

Beverly poured her batter into a loaf pan and slid the pan onto a rack in the oven. "Forty-five minutes," she said. She smiled with cheerful seduction. "Then banana bread and me."

Fritz liked friendly sex. Liked being married. So much easier than his younger days when he sized up every woman as a potential conquest.

He carried his garment bag upstairs. The sun shone here, too, tracking through the spacious room through panoramic windows on three of the walls. The king-sized bed, bedside tables, and walk-in closet took up most of the fourth wall.

Fritz removed his loafers and walked past the bed into the master bath. He turned on the steam to the shower to let it heat up.

He removed the knife hidden inside a sheath in the left pocket of his trousers.

He removed the holster from his right pocket and the thin laser flashlight tucked into the back of his waistband.

He removed another knife strapped to his right shin.

He had worn his semi-automatic in the Bellagio, but he had already returned that to its hiding place in a holster duct-taped beneath the table just inside the front door.

There were more guns on the second and third floors in various strategic locations.

Oil executives were often kidnapping targets, he explained to Beverly very early on. She accepted it without question. And, Fritz noticed, without what he considered a normal amount of fear.

Beverly liked their life together.

She seemed content to leave it at that.

3

Fritz lay in bed with Beverly sleeping on his outstretched arm. It was early afternoon and the sky was darkening before a storm. Six to eight inches, the forecast said.

Christmas white.

He thought about Alice Kern. He knew little about the girl. He had seen her photo among all the others he routinely got about the Agency. He remembered her looking about mid-twenties. She was a low-level analyst.

Daughter of Will Kern. That might matter. Should, since Fritz Zimholt didn't believe in coincidence.

Ingelene would find out more. How the Kern girl had killed the assassin. Why she was being moved to the Aviary. What job they had for her there. How the girl fit into everything else.

Including whether she had any connection to the

extraordinary young woman Fritz had heard about at the Aviary. He didn't believe in coincidence.

Flakes of snow began to fall. Fritz pulled the thick down comforter up higher to cover his bare shoulders. The house was warm, but the view was cold. Beverly slumbered on.

Fritz's father never wanted to live in snow. Not once they came to the States. Their ship landed in New York and it took three years before they could leave, but by the time Fritz was nine the family moved to California.

He had a younger sister and brother by then, both born as American citizens, while he had to wait until his parents became citizens before he could be naturalized through them. He knew no English when he came over. At six years old he learned it faster than both his parents.

They had endured five winters in West Berlin after the war ended. Five Christmases with barely any food. Five Christmases with very little coal for heat, with only runty potatoes and wild mushrooms and whatever else they could scrounge for their Christmas dinner.

It had been the Americans who saved them. After the war, Germany was divided by the victors into four separate zones. The Soviets controlled one, the Americans, British, and French the other three.

The city of Berlin was divided, too. West and East. Soviets controlled the East.

Fritz's family lived in the American zone. But they heard. They knew. Everyone did. They all knew the Soviets were brutal. As brutal as some in the German army had been to others.

The Soviets beat and imprisoned at will, no need for any real reason. They starved the German citizens under their control. They punished them for what their leaders had done, even though ordinary citizens like Fritz's parents wanted no part of Hitler or his disgusting ideas.

Then came the day when the Soviets blocked off road and train access to all of Berlin, even the western side. Before then the Americans and British had regularly transported food and coal and medicine to help the German people survive.

Now nothing could get through.

People died. People died every day. Fritz had a little brother then, just a baby, who died during the winter of the blockade. His mother nearly died, too.

Fritz's father, forced to be a soldier along with millions of other young German men, came back from the war a different and hardened man. He had been a math tutor before, but that skill did him no good during the war or those years after.

Learning to fight. To use a gun and a knife. To kill if he had to. To steal and lie for his family. Those were the skills required.

Fritz's father did things to save his family that would have seemed unthinkable to a gentle man like him before. But desperation does that. Fritz knew of desperation himself.

Then the Americans had saved them.

Fritz moved Beverly off his arm and got out of bed and dressed. He put on thick wool socks, warm sweat pants, a long-sleeved T-shirt and a sweater on top.

Then he quietly descended the stairs. Unlocked the door to his office. Turned up the heat on the wall thermostat before sitting down at his desk.

He had a view from here, too, out toward a different line of peaks. The sky had darkened into early dusk and snow fell heavily now. Fritz was glad to be inside.

He unlocked a drawer on the left side of his desk. He opened it only a few times a year when he felt sentimental, and especially, like now, near Christmas.

He removed what looked like a few layers of faded red flannel cloth. He set them on the desk in front of him and peeled away the top layer.

Protected in various folds of cloth over the years were the metal ornaments his father had once made. Like other soldiers in December 1944, he had been given leave from the German army to return home for Christmas. It had been a scheme to keep up morale. It created a generation of German children born nine months later.

The soldiers all had to make their way home however they could. Fritz's father walked. Across countryside, fields, roads, destroyed and intact towns, walking for days and days to spend Christmas with his parents and siblings and wife.

In a potato field he stopped to dig up some to bring home. And there at the far edge of the field, lying in the dirt, were the remnants of a downed plane.

It was American. Fritz's father could see the markings. He had only a small knapsack with him and it was already full of potatoes and his clothes and some water, but he managed to make room for a few broken strips of metal he scrounged from the airplane's wing.

In another day he made it home. He planted the seed to create Fritz that very night. And then he secretly took his airplane metal and a nail he pulled from the wall and made presents for his family.

He scratched out the shapes with the nail and then used his knife to cut them. Five stars and three moons. Flat, smooth, shiny ornaments made from the wing of an enemy plane.

Fritz had all of them now. They had come with his parents over the Atlantic. The ornaments had hung on his family's Christmas tree every single year.

Fritz never hung them on a tree of his own.

They were too important for that. Too important to have to explain. What they meant to his father. To his mother. To Fritz. Even his two younger siblings would never understand. They had only lived in America. They never knew what the Soviets were like.

Fritz examined the edges, so carefully cut with his father's knife. He could still see a few of the scratches once made by a nail so his father could follow the line.

That terrible winter of the Soviet blockade Fritz understood what it felt like to starve. To be cold every minute of every hour. To be afraid. To know he would die.

And then the Americans had saved him. Saved his family. Saved his people.

The Americans did not go through the blockade, they went above it. Flew supplies into the small Berlin airport, plane after plane bringing food and medicine and coal. Not enough, never enough, but with rationing, the Germans could at least survive.

And some of the airmen even dropped sweets for the children as they flew overhead. Whenever Fritz and his friends saw a plane give the signal by tilting its wings side to side, they scampered out as quickly as they could to retrieve the precious falling bundles of chocolates and candy and chewing gum.

People lived. Eventually the Soviets gave in and freed the roads and the trains and allowed the Germans to survive again.

And then a few years later they built the Berlin wall, but Fritz and his family were already gone by then. Finally after years of waiting it was their turn to win the lottery for immigration visas to America.

Beverly was from California. Her parents were American. She could never understand what these metal ornaments meant.

Fritz pressed his thumb against the sharp point of one of the crescent moons. He traced his finger along the edge of the moon's perfectly curved spine. Such precise work from his mathematician father with such crude tools to make it.

Fritz thought of the gaudy three-dimensional stars hanging from the ceiling of the Bellagio. There was no beauty there. Nothing personal. No one had wept when they were given. Those stars were disposable. Replaceable. Absolutely meaningless.

Fritz sighed. He still missed his father. His mother had

died ten years before him, so that memory was already fading. But he could still see his father sitting in his sagging brown recliner, oxygen tubes in his nose, the broad smile Fritz could never resist, the gentle grip of his arthritic hands. Even in the nursing home, his father had always wanted his own Christmas tree. A small one on the table beneath the window, decorated with lights and his wartime ornaments.

Fritz carefully laid the stars and moons back inside the cloth. He folded the flannel on top of them and returned them to his drawer and locked it.

What makes a man what he is? Fritz sometimes wondered. The qualities of his character. His values. His hatred. His loves.

On a cold snowy day in Berlin he watched a Soviet soldier rape a young girl. She might have been seven or eight. Afterward the soldier smashed her head against a brick wall and her blood reddened the whitened street.

Fritz was young, too. Just five. Too young to do anything other than run tell his parents the girl was dead.

He saw his baby brother, Matthias, take his last breath.

He saw his mother wasting away, barely with enough strength left to lift her own arms.

He saw horrors he refused to think of anymore. People needed meat.

He felt the unending pain of a hunger that went on and on. Even now, an old man, he sometimes felt like crying when he tasted delicious food. What he wouldn't have given in his childhood for this slice of rosemary bread or this juicy pear or this bite of roast chicken or this one simple cracker with cheese.

He saw his father's pride when he brought out his ornaments every year and carefully hung them on his tree.

He saw his father's despair those years in Germany. His joy when they all screamed to each other on the deck of the ship because they could finally see the Statue of Liberty.

Fritz knew which country was good.

An American plane had been shot down over his homeland and the men aboard it had probably died. Fritz thanked those men. The ornaments were a memorial to them and to the weary German soldier who had scrounged those bits of metal and crafted gifts for the family he missed.

American planes had smuggled food into his city and he ate well on the nights they did. He thanked those men. They didn't have to save Germans. He would have understood if they refused to.

Fritz remembered the years after he came to America, the packages his parents would send back to their families in Germany. Chocolate bars. Bags of sugar. Large blue cans of Maxwell House coffee. Things the German people still couldn't get. Boxed up once a year for Christmas, mailed across the water like packages dropping from the sky.

So yes, he had chosen his allegiance.

And his enemy had chosen itself.

He understood that a country's actions were not the same as the people living their ordinary lives.

He also understood that only the people themselves could destroy the ones doing harm.

Whether she realized it or not, Alice Kern, mid-twenties, low-level analyst, daughter of Will Kern, had destroyed one dangerous part of a larger lethal organism that was doing the world enormous harm.

Fritz Zimholt thanked that girl.

And when the time was right, and if it was in his power, he would help her destroy the rest.

~

THE AVIARY

1

―――――

"You're going to want to keep an open mind," Ted Whitling said.

Alice Kern walked beside him across a bright stretch of asphalt toward a pair of airplane hangars in the near distance. Behind her was the jet that had landed only minutes before, carrying Alice, Ted, and Alice's new bodyguard, a tall quiet agent named Santos.

Santos must have felt she was safe here, Alice thought, because he had immediately left her, walked off in another direction toward the main building that seemed to hold the main activity.

Alice glanced at the man striding beside her. Medium height, compact and solid, mid-thirties, she guessed, maybe ten years older than she was. He wore khaki trousers, brown suede loafers, and a short-sleeved dark blue button-down shirt. No jacket, no tie.

She was dressed even more casually, since whoever

had bagged up some of her clothes the day before from her now off-limits apartment hadn't left her with much choice. Jeans, sneakers, and a plain white short-sleeved T-shirt under her black fleece vest. No makeup on her dark brown face, her long brown hair pulled back into a pony-tail, she knew the overall effect made her look younger than her twenty-six years. It didn't help that she was so small she could easily pass for a high school student.

"An open mind about what?" she asked. A jet took off to her right, surprisingly quiet. Also much smaller than she was used to seeing. She watched it quickly gain height and go.

"I'd like your help with someone," said Ted. "I think it might play to your skills."

My skills.

Alice doubted he meant her skills as an analyst. She had worked for the Agency for less than a year and had never attracted any higher-ups' attention. That was how she wanted it. She showed up every day, worked hard, went home and worked harder still on a project all her own.

But that project had bled over to her professional life, and had attracted more attention than she expected. Within the last thirty-one hours two men had tried to kill her: one in her apartment, one in a bookstore. Alice had killed both of them instead: one with a gun, one with her bare hands.

She suspected it was this last fact that led Ted Whitling to suddenly take interest.

She still wasn't clear on who he was. He seemed to

have a supervisory role, but no one had explicitly said it. He had enough rank to score a private jet. Beyond that, Alice was still trying to piece together what she could.

They were in Nevada. She knew that much. The flight from San Diego might have taken a few hours on a commercial flight, but the private jet had gotten them there in a little over an hour.

Now the mid-morning air felt warm and dry. Comfortable for just a few days before Christmas.

Another jet took off. Alice could smell the tinge of fumes, faint, but there. Her stomach felt uncomfortably empty. What she needed was coffee. Maybe a piece of toast. Maybe that's where Santos had gone.

Alice wasn't at her best and she knew it. She felt tired and edgy. She hadn't slept well in the hotel the night before—in part because she'd already been warned that this man she had only briefly been introduced to would be picking her up early and taking her on a mysterious trip.

"It's just temporary," Gina, one of the Agency investigators had said. She was lying in a hospital bed at the time, recovering from the knife wound the assassin had managed to give her before Alice could ward him off.

"You need to get out of town for a while," said Gina. "We'd be stupid to keep you here."

Alice couldn't argue with that, but she still resented not being let in on her own loop. She was used to secrets, but it was her job to uncover them. To not have the major facts about her own situation—the why, who, where, what—felt unsafe in a way she never liked.

Ted was now angling toward the larger hangar on the left. Alice followed, slightly back. She was still trying to assess her surroundings.

The place seemed to be a compound all to itself. "We call it the Aviary," Ted told her as they came in for their descent. "One of our smaller venues. Personnel are limited. Strict security clearances. It's better if a lot of people don't know about this place."

Alice got a good look at it from the jet window. Several long runways at one end with multiple planes coming, going, or waiting. To the west of the airfield a neighborhood of about fifty small houses, two-bedroom at most, and other structures that might be temporary housing.

More structures between the houses and the airfield, maybe offices.

Then the large central building where Santos had gone once they landed. There were a dozen or so carts parked outside it. Other carts were in motion, ferrying people around the compound.

And here, on the north side where she and Ted now walked, were sets of hangars in a variety of sizes, a few of them larger than Alice had ever seen in a commercial airport.

Everything looked new. The buildings, the carts, the planes.

Either new or very well cared for.

On the runway to her right another one of the smaller jets sped past and rose swiftly into the air.

All that quick power, Alice thought, and yet it was so *quiet*.

Maybe the Aviary was a testing area for new kinds of planes. It made sense. There was nothing around the airfield for miles and miles. There was a range of mountains to the north, but no signs of civilization until you got past it.

But then what am I doing here? Alice had no training or knowledge about any of this.

But maybe it was simply the place where they had chosen to hide her. Some compound in the middle of a high desert where no one would think to look.

As long as they gave her access to the files and let her continue her work, Alice didn't care whether she was here or a concrete bunker in Alaska.

But she needed to continue with her work.

If for no other reason than to discover why two different men had tried to kill her within the space of a single morning.

Ted was waiting for her now in the wide open doorway of the hangar. Alice lengthened her stride. The sooner she finished this tour, the faster she could get settled wherever they were going to put her and return to researching the files.

She stood beside Ted and looked inside the hangar. Her eyes took a moment to adjust. There were no overhead lights—at least none that were on—so she could only see as far as the daylight penetrated.

There were two rows of medium-sized jets stretching

far back into darkness. There might be twenty or thirty of them in all.

No one seemed to be around. Alice continued peering into the hangar, waiting for some explanation.

Finally Ted jerked his chin upward. Alice tilted her head and looked.

A figure had moved into view.

A woman with chin-length brown hair. Lanky, thin, wearing black leggings, dark sneakers, and a long-sleeved black top. Alice's age, maybe, although it was hard to tell from this distance.

The woman was overhead, flying.

Flying, although that was impossible.

She swam like a swimmer in air. Her arms alternating in a freestyle crawl, feet pattering behind her with perfect form.

Then she switched. Did a mid-air horizontal roll like she was a dolphin lolling on her back, then came out of the roll into a butterfly stroke, stretching her arms wide out to her side, arcing them forward over her head, and kicking her feet together a moment later like a swimmer in the Olympics.

Alice's head felt light.

She had to sit down. She lowered herself onto the cold concrete floor and pinched her fingers against her eyes.

It wasn't real.

She could feel her mind grasping for some anchor. Searching for something to hold. Forcing herself to accept. Just like she'd had to learn six years ago.

Is this real?

This is real.

Are they really dead?

They're really dead.

She used to have a vivid imagination.

One her mother, in particular, used to share.

The two of them loved any stories about magic or superheroes. They read to each other and watched movies all throughout Alice's childhood. Even into high school and the beginning of college, at least once a month, Movie Night. Kung Fu Theater. Superheroes. Wizards.

Alice glanced up again. The woman was nearly out of view, swimming her way toward the back of the hangar.

Mama would love this, Alice thought. Dr. Aurora Kern would have gazed up at that strange, impossible sight and would have been awestruck.

And also immensely delighted.

But Alice felt worried, not delighted. She needed facts, truth. Otherwise this might be just another story in her head.

"How is it even possible?" she asked Ted.

He crouched down next to her.

"We don't know yet," he said. "We'd like to find out."

"But… who is she? Where did she come from?"

"Her name is Marnie Stemple," said Ted. "At least we think that's her name. She's not very forthcoming. She hasn't exactly warmed up to us yet."

A burst of laughter escaped Alice's lips. Even though none of this was funny.

"There are people," Ted said. "She's not the only one.

You just never hear about them. We're very good at keeping it secret."

Suddenly something made sense.

Back in the hospital, Gina had given Alice a series of five comic books from her own personal collection.

At the time it seemed so frivolous.

"Do your research," Gina told her. "It's what you're good at. You might actually find some parts of those useful."

The covers had featured a medieval-looking woman warrior with long black hair. She held a sword. She protected a child. There was a helicopter behind her on one of the covers, and then the last issue showed her wearing an enormous pair of wings.

Wings. Gina knew. There really was some woman at the Aviary who could fly. How many other people knew? Why were they sharing the secret with Alice?

The comics were in Alice's bag right now. Back on the jet, as far as she knew. She hadn't bothered looking at any of them the night before. Why should she? She had work to do.

And she was done with make-believe. Done with her childish, girlhood fantasies.

A gunman had shot them out of her when Alice was twenty and she saw the scene of the carnage playing endlessly on the news. She didn't have to wait for the strangers who came to her apartment to tell her her parents were dead. She already knew. In her heart she knew.

And yet her mind refused to accept it for a painfully long time.

They're coming back.

There's been a mistake.

I just dreamed it, it never really happened.

Other college juniors were still young. Alice wasn't anymore. There were a lot of things she wasn't anymore: Pre-med. In love. A daughter. Happy. Hopeful. Naïve.

One day she woke up and really knew: They were gone now. And no amount of magic or wishing would bring them back.

When she finally returned to college, it was to study something else. Anything that could help her understand. Psychology. Criminal justice. Cyber investigation. Forensics.

She graduated with honors, but she still didn't understand. She even took philosophy and religion classes on good versus evil and whether the universe was just.

And now she worked. Toward the only tangible goal of finding every single person with any connection to her parents' death and bringing them before the law.

Seeing them tried. Imprisoned. Even killed.

Alice felt a constant rage underneath the surface each and every day. And so she worked. And made sure that no one knew how personal her research really was.

This, right here, this real-life fantasy of a woman flying back and forth in an airplane hangar on a remote base in Nevada—it was nothing but a distraction.

And yet.

Alice could feel the tug on her heart. From a mother who still sometimes lived there.

Aurora Kern would have traveled across the earth to get to see something as amazingly impossible as this. She was a scientist, but she would have believed. She wouldn't try to deny something she could see with her own eyes.

Even Will Kern, Alice's father, far more of a skeptic, would have looked up at the woman doing freestyle through the air and would have managed at least a "Huh." He would have smiled. Shaken his head. Kissed his wife and squeezed his daughter's shoulder and told them both, "You're up."

It was what he said when he didn't want to answer the door or the phone or go to a party instead of stay home and read. *You're up.*

But later he would have wanted to hear their full report.

Alice cleared her throat. She needed water. Coffee. A clear head. Facts. She offered her hand and let Ted pull her to her feet.

She brushed off the back of her jeans and gazed upward again. Marnie was just coming back into view. Alice wondered how many times the woman flew back and forth and back and forth. Like a goldfish swimming circles in a bowl.

Alice let out a sigh before she could stop it. "All right," she told Ted Whitling. "What do you need me to do?"

2

"Marnie?" Ted called. "Can you come down here for a minute? I want you to meet someone."

He didn't often do that.

Ted checked on her a few times a day, or sent others to do it when he was away.

But Marnie wasn't expected to talk to them. Ted must have told everyone not to bother her.

She had been at the Aviary—what a wonderful name, what a wonderful place—for coming on two weeks now.

She could fly sixteen hours a day if she wanted. All Ted asked was that she sleep a good amount and take regular breaks to eat and drink.

He even sent people to the hangar with food. Most of them understood what she liked, just chips and nuts and other snacks, apples or cherries, nothing heavy, but there had been that one gray-haired woman last week who brought Marnie a turkey sandwich.

Turkey.

Marnie looked at the woman with horror. Still the lady didn't seem to understand.

"I can't eat *that*," Marnie said. "It's a bird."

Then she took off and flew for the next two hours straight just to get the image of it out of her head.

Ted had been bringing the food since then, but maybe this new girl beside him was the replacement. She looked Hawaiian. A sporty girl of maybe twenty.

And now Ted wanted Marnie to meet her.

An annoyance, but it would be over quickly. Then they'd go back to leaving her alone.

It was the first time in eleven years that Marnie could do whatever she wanted.

No job she had to go to. No sneaking off every hour just to fit in ten minutes of flying.

The compulsion was already soothed. Knowing she could fly anytime took away the itch. The nagging, incessant need.

She slept for three whole hours at a time now. The longest since she was seventeen. Ted's people kept records, she knew—she assumed someone was always watching, they were government people, after all—but Marnie was also keeping track of herself.

Sleep was something she longed for. Like a childhood taste of something her mother used to make. For over a decade she just assumed she would never see it again. That she would live out her days, however long or short they were, with only naps, punctuated by flight, then another nap, every night of her life.

But here she languished in bed. So much flight, her body was tired and slept naturally. She didn't awaken to every sound, even though this place was still new and strange.

Ted said they would protect her and she was close to believing it was true.

There were still moments. Someone sticking out a hand too fast, wanting to shake hers she had to realize, not grab her.

People watching her. Noticing her. But not interfering in any way.

She wanted to get used to that.

But Marnie also knew in the reserve of her mind that none of this was for free. The world didn't work that way. People didn't. The feds, certainly not.

They wanted something from her. No one had asked yet, but she knew that day was coming. Let her settle in, she could imagine them saying whenever they discussed her case. Don't startle her. She'll run.

She'll fly.

And she would. Marnie already had a plan. She always had a plan.

They followed her on the flights she took outside the hangar, the dawn and sunset flights out over the mountains.

Those tiny silent jets. Tracking her. Probably filming, she had to assume.

But no trackers *on* her. Nothing on her clothes or under her skin.

If she had to escape, she could do it under cover of

darkness once they got used to seeing her sleep.

She landed gently on top of the closest plane and then hopped lightly onto the floor.

The young woman smiled at her, although Marnie thought she detected something else there. Uncertainty. That was as close as she could call it.

Ted introduced them. "Marnie, this is Alice Kern. She's going to be staying with us for a while. She's under our protection."

Marnie thought Alice looked at him with surprise. But she recovered quickly enough and held out her hand. "Hi. Nice to meet you."

Marnie jerked back a little from the girl's firm grip. Not what she was expecting. Now that she had a better look at Alice's face, she wondered if maybe she underestimated her age. There was a weariness at the edge of her eyes that Marnie could sometimes see in her own.

"Alice doesn't know anybody yet," Ted said. "I told her she could hang out here for a while. I need to go get her room set up. Do you mind keeping her company for a few minutes?"

Without waiting for an answer, Ted jogged off toward the Hub.

"Under their protection?" Marnie asked. "Do you have some... power?" She hated calling it that, but hated it worse when they called it a gift. She didn't want to fly, she had no choice.

And the idea that this young woman might have a similar problem made Marnie feel hopeful. Maybe she really wasn't alone.

"No," Alice answered. She hesitated a moment before saying more. "I'm an analyst with the Agency. I had some trouble yesterday. Two men tried to kill me."

Marnie's pulse jumped. She almost took off flying right then. It was part of the impulse, and one she valued —fight or flight, and she always chose flight. It had protected her well over the years so far.

"What happened?" she asked.

"I killed them both," said Alice.

Matter-of-factly, as if it were nothing. Marnie could feel sweat start to bead on her face.

"But the Agency thinks it's too dangerous for me right now," Alice said. "So I'm here to train for a few days while they investigate it some more."

"Train... what?" Marnie asked. Suddenly she had a suspicion. The timing was too convenient.

"Myself," said Alice. "It's been a while since I've done martial arts. I need to get back in form."

Marnie's heartbeat stuttered.

"What are your concerns?" Ted Whitling had asked her that first day they met, two weeks ago.

"Look at me," she answered. *"I'm not tough. I can't fight. I don't know martial arts..."*

Oh, he was good.

Alice held out her hand again. "It was very nice to meet you. But I'm starving. Can I come find you later?"

"Sure," said Marnie. She could hear the uncertainty in her own voice.

Alice smiled and then turned and walked away.

Marnie ran a few steps back into the hangar and flapped her arms into flight.

Then she pivoted in the air to watch Alice. That small young woman had killed two men? How?

It was a set-up, Marnie thought. It might not even be true. She knew what they wanted from her.

She couldn't trust the feds.

"Whitling said you'd want these." The short, tawny-haired airman sat across from Alice in the mess hall and passed a thumb drive beneath the rim of her plate.

She had just had a late breakfast of pancakes and coffee and was feeling almost right again.

The name patch on the airman's gray flight suit said "Camper."

"Arnie Camper," he told her, thrusting out his hand. "I fly the Snack Packs."

"The what?"

"The SPs," he said. "Stealth Pods. Snack Packs. You've probably seen them."

"Those tiny jets?" Alice guessed.

"One-seaters," Camper confirmed. "Recon. I've been following Ms. Stemple on her mountain flights. Whitling said you'd want to see the footage."

"Oh, yes," said Alice. "Thank you." She pocketed the thumb drive in her fleece vest.

"Grub's not bad," said Camper, indicating her empty plate. "Gotta go. Send word if you got any questions." He was off as fast as he'd arrived.

Alice walked back to the guest quarters where they'd put her, a small single room in a complex of about thirty. The building was made of plain concrete, with exterior doors that opened onto a stark asphalt courtyard like some military version of a motel.

Back in her modest room Alice set her laptop on the laminate-topped metal desk and waited for it to boot up. There was no closet in there, just a footlocker at the bottom of her bed. She had unpacked her garbage bag full of clothes and put the comics under her pillow. She would read them later. No one needed to notice them if they came into her room while she was gone.

She inserted the thumb drive in the laptop and brought up the video files.

"Seventh December, oh-seven-twenty-three hours," she heard Camper's voice say. "Subject in flight."

There was Marnie, filling enough of the screen that Alice wondered how close Camper was. Marnie didn't seem to notice any aircraft flying above her. Who knew how far the zoom on the camera worked.

It wasn't until Marnie did one of her horizontal rolls that Alice could see her smile.

She paused the video. Reversed. Watched again.

One of her psych courses had been about people's ability

to hide their emotions. There are certain things you're trained to look for: the amount of creasing below and at the edge of the eyes. The ratio of lip curvature to overall width of the mouth. Comparisons to animal faces, like when dogs' tongues hang between their teeth in a relaxed kind of panting versus the wider "smile" of a dog who is stressed.

Marnie Stemple was relaxed.

No, Marnie was in *bliss*.

Unguarded. Serene. At peace.

And then a moment, so fast it would have been easy to miss: Marnie looking upward, peeking, almost.

She knew the Snack Pack was there.

Maybe even felt… comforted by that.

But she clearly wasn't performing for the camera. She rolled back onto her belly and continued doing her swimmer's crawl and then some butterfly, and every now and then she rolled onto her back to look up before rolling to her belly again.

Alice quickly wrote herself some notes.

Then she sped through other footage on the thumb drive, looking for the takeoff. Most of the time Camper didn't seem to pick her up until she was already flying. But there, one morning, a little earlier. 07:14, the time stamp said.

Marnie leaving one of the rooms in the same complex as Alice's, it looked like, just a few doors down. She zoomed in on the number to confirm it.

The video showed just a first hint of light outside. Marnie zipped up a dark brown jacket.

Then she took a few long strides. Swung her arms in a few circles. Warming up, it looked like.

Then a little trot. A hop, another hop, the way Alice had seen long jumpers do it. Then arms out to her sides, starting the movement up and down, and finally the momentary crouch and spring upward while her arms flapped at speed.

Alice stared in wonder.

Replayed it. Slowly. Mapped it out movement by movement.

Then she smiled to herself.

A distraction, yes, but one her mind felt excited to embrace after all.

Huh, Alice thought. *You're up.*

4

Marnie donned her light jacket and pulled on a pair of socks. The temperature in the hangar was cool, but it was uniform. The outside weather didn't seem to affect it. She could even fly barefoot in here some of the time.

But there was wind over the mountains, and her ankles felt cold if she didn't cover them. She pulled her black canvas sneakers back on and hurried to her feet.

This was the best time—the absolute *best time*. Better, even, than dawn.

Something about the late afternoon wind patterns here made her feel like she was flying a kite. The way she could catch a gust with the tips of her hands and then glide on it for miles.

The purple and orange sunset lighting the sky to her left.

The personal escort high above her where they must have thought she couldn't see.

She knew this couldn't last. Knew it from the moment Ted Whitling came back to her apartment a day after their first interview and told her he had a solution.

"What do I have to do?" she asked him.

"Nothing," he said. "It's what we can do for you."

Salesman talk. Fed talk. Of course they wanted something from her. She could fly, of course they wanted that. Make her into a weapon. Or a courier. Something she had no intention of doing.

But until then, she would squeeze out every moment.

It was the safest she had felt since she lost her mother at seventeen.

Food. Sleep. Flying for miles in the open air every dawn and dusk. Flying for hours every day, as much as she wanted, free finally to live.

But Alice was the first sign. They were going to try to make something of Marnie.

Weaponize her. Teach her to fight.

But not right now. Not for as long as she could delay it.

Right now she only had to fly.

5

Alice asked at the front office how to access the movies she needed. Then she returned to her room with a Hub-issued viewer and the code to bring up any film she wanted.

She kicked off her sneakers and propped up her pillow and settled comfortably onto her bed. The bedspread was scratchy, military, but the pillow was pleasantly soft.

Alice took a deep breath.

Then she clicked on the first movie.

It had been a long time since she had allowed herself to watch any of these.

A long time since she had wanted to.

They felt like home movies, even though they were films made in Hong Kong.

She knew the instant Ted gave her her assignment that this was where she had to start.

Martial arts fights balancing on the thin branches of bamboo trees.

Aerial moves supported by hidden wires. *Wire-fu,* some people called it. The impossibly high leaps and suspension while doing the splits and kicking two different opponents in the head at the same time.

The light footfalls of someone sprinting over the smooth surface of a lake.

All moves Alice and both her parents had loved watching together on movie nights, although Alice's father was always the voice of reason.

"That's a useless attack," he'd remind them. "Unless you can figure out how to hover four feet off the ground."

Alice had found someone who could.

She had to pause every now and then, overcome with tears.

God, she missed them.

She could be spending this time following more leads, uncovering the network that had paid for their killer.

But this was just for a day. She would get back to her research tomorrow.

She particularly liked the movies starring the young Chinese actress who was small, like her. Small but powerful. Well-placed kicks. Expert handling of weapons. Proper form to all of her strikes and blocks.

If Alice really could teach Marnie to defend herself.

"Help her feel safe," Ted Whitling had said back in the hangar this morning. "Show her what to do."

Alice had some ideas.

And it was a task that spoke to her heart.

Her Filipino uncles had taught her martial arts since she was a child. Alice's parents had met at their dojo. Fighting was in Alice's blood.

By the time she was in high school, her uncles let her take over teaching all of the other girls in the dojo. She even taught the grown women.

She wanted them all to be strong. Smart. Safe.

And yes, she wanted that for Marnie too.

She could see how vulnerable Marnie was. How easy it would be for someone to catch her and hurt her.

"She won't trust you," Ted Whitling had warned.

"Good," said Alice. "That's a good instinct."

6

Alice was on her third movie when her growling stomach convinced her to take a break. It was already dark outside.

She followed the lighted walkway to the mess hall, her mind still in a bamboo forest under speckled light where her favorite Chinese heroine clung to one of the swaying thick green stalks and fought off her opponents with her free hand.

No good, Alice reminded herself. Marnie wouldn't have a free hand. She needed both of them for flying. But she could copy some of the heroine's kicks.

Alice slid a tray along the metal rails of the food line and thought about Marnie's arms. They were clearly strong enough to keep herself aloft. But what about the rest of her body?

"Beans?" the server asked.

"Sure." The man on the kitchen side of the food line asked her other questions and Alice nodded without really hearing.

She carried her tray back to the same table and exact seat where she'd eaten breakfast that morning. Alice liked routine. It freed up her mind to think of more important things.

She looked down at her plate, surprised by how much food was there. She sampled a few bites, then lifted her head and finally looked around.

Across the room she spied someone familiar. A tall, grave-looking Hispanic man. Alice gave him a quizzical look. He picked up his plate and came over.

"Everything fine?" Santos asked her.

"I didn't know where you went."

"Whitling's orders," Santos said. "The optics."

"What optics?"

"Have to ask him." Santos gave her a polite nod, then carried his plate to another table where he sat down alone once more and continued eating.

Is he still protecting me?

Alice assumed he was still armed with a gun and knives, just like he had been the day before. But maybe she didn't need protection here. They must have all sorts of security built in to a place like this.

What optics?

"Ma'am." Arnie Camper seemed to materialize in front of her and took up the same seat he'd briefly occupied that morning. He slipped her another thumb drive.

"Just finished," he said. "Pretty much the same. Still thought you might want it."

"I do. Thanks." She slid it into her vest pocket.

Camper nodded in approval at her plate heaped high with beans, rice, two corn tortillas, guacamole, and chips. On a separate side plate waited a slice of chocolate cake.

Camper was eyeing that in particular.

"Want it?" Alice asked, pushing the plate across.

"No, thanks," Camper said. "Got weigh-in in the morning."

"Weigh-in?"

"Once a week," he said. "Like jockeys. Gotta keep it slim." He patted his taut belly. "No one over five-six either. Snack Packs don't like it." He grinned. "And here I worried I was too small. Evening, ma'am." He hopped back up to his feet.

"You can call me Alice."

"Enjoy that cake, Alice."

She watched him go. Thought about what he said.

It would be true of Marnie too.

She couldn't carry too much weight on her body. Her proportions had to remain the way they were. Good upper body strength, but not a lot of bulk from the waist down.

Strong legs, but not too much muscle. Even though Marnie kicked her feet behind her sometimes, they didn't seem to propel her forward. Everything was from her arms. More like a rock climber relying on her fingers and forearms to pull her up than like a swimmer who needed powerful thighs.

But there was one place the legs mattered.

If Alice could help her with the takeoff.

That would be something. Straight up without the need to run and take those first few leaps.

Straight up like a helicopter instead of that diagonal acceleration like a jet.

It would help her get away much faster. That could matter in a dangerous situation.

Alice went back to thinking about Marnie's arms. Whatever Marnie did, she'd have to protect them. She couldn't expose them to being broken or otherwise impaired. So there was no use teaching her to punch or chop.

It all had to be her legs. Take off, gain height, then kick.

Kick the hell out of people.

Just like the young Chinese woman in Alice's favorite movies. Strong and slim. Strong and light.

Marnie could do this.

Alice took a few more bites of everything on her plate and a couple of forkfuls of cake. She grabbed a few bottles of fizzy water on her way out and asked how early she'd find coffee.

The mess hall worker rewarded her with a mini coffee pot all her own and enough supplies to take her through a couple of days.

Alice carried her treasure back to her room and restarted the bamboo forest fight.

By the time she finished watching the remaining two movies it was late, almost eleven. But Ted Whitling had given her his cell phone number and said to call any time. She took him at his word.

"I'll need a few things," Alice said.

She gave him a list of equipment.

"You'll have them by tomorrow," Ted said.

arnie's morning flight had been perfect.

Cool air, a slight breeze, a golden winter sun rising over the horizon.

She stalled several times on purpose. Stopped moving at all. Just to feel the soft air holding her, even for just a few seconds, before she had to flap again to stay aloft.

Sometimes the air felt delicious. When she lived in humid climates some days she could barely stand it. That wet, suffocating feeling of air almost too heavy to stay on top of. It was why she preferred staying in the west. Everything felt milder, even when there was snow. Snow and sunny days she could bear. Icy snow and wet air and gray skies made her feel stiff and frozen to her bones.

As she neared her hangar, she saw activity below. There was a cargo plane parked in front of the hangar next door. Its ramp had been lowered, and a dozen or so men unloaded metal bars and various rolled up bundles and other pieces of equipment. They carried them into the hangar on the right.

Marnie didn't know those men. Her heartbeat sped. The lazy feeling to the morning was gone. She landed behind the pair of hangars where no one could see her and came around the front on foot.

The hangar on the right was practically empty. All the planes that had been stored there were gone.

Instead there were metal parts all lined up on the floor and a large roll of what looked like dark green canvas.

There was another roll of what looked like netting.

Marnie's pulse spiked.

They throw it over you. Capture you. Hold you on the ground forever.

She started backing away.

"Morning, Miss," one of the men said. He smiled and she took off at a run.

She barely waited to reach her own hangar before flapping her arms to get off the ground.

She flew hard. Fast. Her breath rushing out in gasps.

I have to leave, she told herself in a panic. *Right **now**.*

She never should have trusted these people.

You can't leave. They'll follow you.

They would. They followed her every day. She had seen the jet above her just fifteen minutes ago.

Then tonight, she promised herself. *I'll leave tonight.*

Yes. As soon as it's dark. Do my regular flight, pretend I'm going to bed, then leave when no one is watching.

Go where?

She could make it to Utah easily by morning. Not to

the mountains, too cold in December, maybe Moab. She had looked it up once, put it on her list. Or on to Arizona again, maybe someplace on the border like Douglas.

It was dove season now. She remembered. Dove season until the first week in January.

Someplace else then. Someplace. But not here. She had to go.

8

Alice brewed a cup of coffee with water from her bathroom sink. She had awakened feeling guilty about how much time she wasted the day before.

She would start looking at photos even before breakfast. She felt slightly hungry, but she needed answers more.

Who was the man in the bookstore? The one who had stabbed the investigator Gina and then attacked Alice with the same knife?

Black hair. Glasses. She had to imagine him without the glasses. Hefty build. Maybe five-ten, around two hundred twenty pounds.

Age? Early thirties, maybe.

Hairy arms. She had noticed that but forgotten until now. Clean shaven, but with that kind of latent facial hair that probably started coming back in by the end of the day.

Teeth? Nothing noteworthy. Clothes? Black jacket, maybe.

I should be better than this. Details mattered.

Alice knew who the first assassin was, the one who broke into her apartment earlier that same morning, because she had already seen him in photos. His name was Danic. She didn't know who he worked for. Not yet. But he was part of a collection of men she'd been tracking in photos for a while.

But not the black-haired man. She had never seen him before, either in person or in photos. At least she didn't think so.

She logged into her Agency account and checked messages. Ted Whitling had warned her not to communicate with anyone. The fact that Danic knew where Alice lived and the second man followed her to the bookstore meant there might be someone within the Agency itself who was feeding information to Danic's group.

It was an unsettling fact to consider.

The idea that one of Alice's own co-workers might be working for the wrong side.

And since there were more wrong sides than any one analyst could manage to cover, it meant Alice was currently fighting blind. The enemy might be someone she had never even heard of.

Watching Alice, watching others, reporting on their research.

She couldn't let that stop her. She pulled up the files she had been looking into most recently. The ones where she'd seen Danic's picture. She spent the next two hours going through each group shot, meticulously searching for the black-haired assassin.

Nothing.

She logged off and stood and stretched her back. She needed more coffee and some food.

She brushed her teeth again and splashed some water on her face, then put her hair back in a ponytail. She dressed in workout pants and a red T-shirt and zipped her black fleece vest on top.

She locked her room and walked along the path to the mess hall.

And thought about the lie she'd told Marnie.

About needing to train again in martial arts. Get herself back in form.

Why had she said that?

It just came to her in the moment. But it wasn't a horrible idea.

Obviously her instincts were still there. Even though she hadn't been in the dojo for years. It was one of the things she lost. Another thing to miss, even though she could have gone back any time.

She was always afraid it would break her heart.

But her body missed it. The movements, so like a dance. The snap and sharpness of chops and blocks, the smooth rapidity of punches, the roundness of parries and redirections all to protect and save.

And kicks. She needed to practice her kicks.

In case Marnie was willing to learn them.

There were a few people eating in the mess hall, only a

fraction of the dinner crowd. No familiar faces. No Santos or Camper.

But as soon as she sat down with a plate of eggs and toast and another cup of coffee, she could see Ted Whitling coming toward her from the entrance.

He paused and turned to the food line to get his own cup of coffee. Then he settled beside her at the table.

"Everything's ready," he said.

"Good. Thank you."

"How are you coming with her?"

Alice shrugged. "I can't rush it."

"I understand," Ted said. "But it would be good if you could start soon. You never know."

"Never know what?" she asked. "What are you planning for her?"

"I'm not sure," he said. "We're waiting to see."

"But you just want her to know how to defend herself," Alice confirmed.

"That's right."

"Okay. I'll head over as soon as I'm done."

Ted got up and left. She noticed he hadn't touched his coffee.

She wondered once more what his exact job was.

And what they really were planning to do with Marnie.

9

After the first half hour of panicked sprinting, Marnie slowed her flying to her normal pace.

She needed to conserve her energy. She would be flying for hours tonight. And flying outdoors, against wind and maybe through weather. A lot more challenging than swimming back and forth at the top of the hangar.

She flew and thought.

These past two weeks had been wonderful. She wouldn't pretend otherwise. Like going to a spa, she imagined, and having no more responsibility than showing up for yoga classes and massages.

The sleep had been so wonderful. It might have been the best part. Three hours at a time felt like the greatest luxury. She was grateful to them for that.

So even though the anger was there, anger that they couldn't just leave her alone, that they lied, that were going to try to force her to do something she didn't want, just like she suspected from the start—even with all of that, Marnie couldn't deny that these last two weeks had been good.

Maybe the best two weeks of her life.

But that couldn't be true, she thought, switching back to butterfly. Not when she'd had all those years with her mother. She just didn't think of it that way back then. She assumed it would go on and on.

And then came the bad time.

There were never any good days after that.

It was close to noon when Marnie heard shouting from the hangar next door.

Not constant, but occasional. Bursts of noise, just one word, something like "HA!" or something close.

A woman's shout. Marnie's nerves tingled.

Another shout, and now she was curious.

She would just peek. Fly from her own ceiling over to the lower ceiling next door. Keep her distance. But see.

The other hangar was different now. Blue padded mats had been laid out in a square taking up a large section of the floor.

There was something else.

A long rectangular trampoline with a sturdy metal base and a tall swath of netting encasing it on every side.

The netting.

Alice was alone in the hangar. Marnie hovered out of sight and watched her.

"HUH!" Alice grunted as she stepped to her right and smashed her elbow against her opposite open hand. Then she glided forward another step, and another, making some circular movements with her hands. She hopped backward and with a "HAH!" kicked her left leg out to the side.

It was fascinating to watch. The maneuvers went on and on. Sometimes graceful and circular, sometimes hard and sharp and fast.

Finally, about ten minutes later, Alice came to a stop. She bowed to some unseen presence, then walked backward off the mat.

Marnie could see the sweat pouring down Alice's face.

But she looked happy.

Or at least satisfied.

Marnie's arms were tired. It was harder to hold herself in place for so long than it was to move forward.

She decided to stay rather than go back to her own hangar.

She slowly descended to the floor.

"What was that?" she asked.

Alice smiled and held up a finger for Marnie to wait while she finished chugging a bottle of water.

"*Kata*," Alice gasped, sounding out of breath. "Bad *kata*, if you want to know the truth. I didn't realize how rusty I am. And out of shape."

She didn't look out of shape at all, but Marnie didn't say so.

"It's supposed to be a perfect version of our forms," Alice went on. "A stylized fight against a perfect opponent who is your exact height and skill level." She laughed. "But I would have lost."

"It looked... hard," Marnie said.

"Some of them are," Alice agreed. "But mostly because I haven't practiced in so long."

She held out an unopened bottle of water to Marnie. "Flying looks harder."

"It depends," Marnie said. She cracked the top and drank. Alice was right to think she was thirsty. "It's mostly that it's just so... constant. I *have* to do it. I don't always want to."

Alice seemed to take that in for a moment. "How long have you been doing it?" she asked.

"Since I was sixteen."

Marnie could see the answer surprised her. "No," she answered the unspoken question. "I wasn't born this way."

"Can I ask you how?" Alice said.

Marnie sighed. "It's a long story. And not a very nice one."

Alice nodded. She didn't press. "Can I show you something?" she asked.

"Okay," Marnie said.

She wondered why she didn't feel more frightened right now. Maybe it was because Alice was alone. Maybe because Alice spoke to her like Marnie wasn't some anomaly, some freak of nature.

Spoke to her like it was just a normal conversation. The way people did when they didn't know Marnie's secret.

But this was new, someone knowing about her and still being fine.

"You probably know they film you flying sometimes,"

said Alice. She walked away from the mats toward the trampoline. Marnie followed.

"Yes," she said. She appreciated the chance to speak truthfully. Appreciated Alice telling the truth herself.

Alice climbed up the little three-rung ladder to the canvas top. She parted the netting to go inside and closed it behind her.

She bounced on the trampoline. She continued bouncing, gaining a little more height each time.

"I looked at some of the footage," Alice said. Her voice staccatoed along with her jumps. "You probably don't want my opinion—you're obviously doing fine—but if you want, I was thinking about your takeoff."

"What do you mean?" Marnie asked.

At the height of her bounces Alice's head was still below the netting, but Marnie could see she could still go higher. Now with each jump Alice added her arms, flapping them the way Marnie did.

"You always run first, right?" Alice called. The trampoline was louder now. "Then you leap?" She jumped and pumped her arms. "But what if you didn't need that much build up? What if you could just start flying from where you stood?"

Marnie watched as Alice's jumps took her higher and higher each time. And all the while Alice pumped her arms up and down as if she had some hope she might actually take off.

"It just takes a little more leg strength," Alice called. "I think the arms would stay the same. I thought you might like to try it like this and see what you think."

Alice stopped flapping her arms. She stopped bouncing and let her legs absorb the tremble of the canvas. Then with a bouncing gait she jogged over to the edge of the trampoline and climbed down.

"You want to try?" Alice asked.

Marnie smiled.

The truth was, she did.

But the truth was more than that, she realized. Although she didn't want Alice to know. It had been so long—*so* long—since anyone had paid her any real attention.

Pathetic, Marnie thought. But at the same time she craved it. More than she could have possibly predicted.

Marnie ascended the little ladder. She could have flown, but now she felt self-conscious. She didn't want to take her running leap.

She had never played on a trampoline, even when she was a kid. She had been in jumping castles at birthday parties, but they were so much squishier underfoot. The canvas of the trampoline felt heavy and solid. Jumping on it didn't feel easy.

"You'll get the rhythm," Alice encouraged. "It's always a little awkward at first."

Marnie felt like that geek at the dance who can't bob at the right time with the music.

"That's it," Alice called. "Take your time. Use your arms to get your balance."

Marnie flapped. Not so much that she'd lift up, but just enough to help gain a little more height and take some of the impact off her legs.

It felt free in a completely different way.

Like flying, but with solid earth beneath her. A regular return to the surface beneath her feet, then up, free again in the air.

"Now try," Alice said. "Straight up. Go."

Marnie closed her eyes so she could feel her way through the movement. Hit the ground, bend the knees, push off, flap, keep flapping.

She could feel herself rise. Her feet didn't come back down this time. She opened her eyes to make sure she wouldn't ram her head against the ceiling.

It was different, so different. Effortless. Like steam rising from a bowl. She grinned down at Alice.

"Good, Marnie!" Alice gave her a short round of applause.

Marnie floated back down to the surface. "My legs feel wobbly," she confessed. "They're not very strong."

"They'll get there," said Alice. "If you just jumped on there a little every day, you'd be surprised how fast they'd improve. But that's probably enough for today. I don't want you to overdo it."

Marnie parted the netting and climbed down.

"Most important question," said Alice. "Do you like it?"

"I do."

Alice smiled. "Perfect. Can I show you something else?"

Marnie nodded. She followed Alice back toward the mats.

"These are just a few ideas," Alice said as she bent over to retrieve the tablet-looking device resting on the floor.

"They're from my favorite movies. I skipped to the best scenes. I really think you could do them."

She turned on the device and handed it to Marnie. "Take a look. There are five of them. Just click the different tabs at the bottom." She stepped away from Marnie, back onto the blue mats. "I'm going to work on my *kata* some more. Take your time."

Alice turned from her and once more gave a short respectful bow to some unseen imaginary observer. Then she stepped gracefully into motion, performing the blocks, kicks, and other moves Marnie watched before. Punctuated every now and then with shouts of "HAH!" as Alice struck some blow against her perfect imaginary opponent.

Marnie backed away to the side of the hangar to watch the whole performance. Alice's face was focused. Intense. Her eyes were hard and fierce. Marnie thought her expression alone would have warned someone away.

And the way she moved, her arms and legs so agile, every move so strong and precise... Marnie could imagine the fight. Could picture Alice winning. It didn't matter how small she was, Alice looked like she could defeat anyone who attacked her.

She must never feel afraid. Why would she? Now it didn't surprise her at all what Alice had told her the day before: that she had killed two men who tried to kill her. Of course she did. What Marnie wouldn't give to feel that safe.

Even though the idea of violence terrified her. Even

just watching Alice now made Marnie's heart beat unnaturally fast.

Alice finished her tenth *kata* and bowed to her invisible opponent. Sweat glistened on her face. She bent down to pick up her water and saw Marnie watching.

Marnie smiled and applauded, just like Alice did after Marnie's takeoff on the trampoline.

Alice grinned. "That time felt better." She gestured toward the device Marnie still held. "What did you think?"

"Oh. I didn't watch it yet."

Alice walked over to the side of the hangar and sat beside Marnie on the floor. "Good," she said. "Then I can watch them again too."

She reached over and pressed the arrow in the center to play.

A young Asian woman, maybe twenty years old, rode a wildly galloping horse. The woman wore a bright blue kimono-looking robe, black wide-legged pants, and short soft-looking black boots.

She looked back behind her, worried. For good reason. A group of men chased her on horseback, all of them carrying swords or spears.

She came to the edge of a cliff. Nowhere to go.

The men caught up. Advanced, weapons lifted. Confident, Marnie could see. They had her.

But with a yell the young woman leapt from her horse and did the splits mid-air. She kicked two men in the head at the same time. She landed, leapt high again, this time kicking away spears aiming for her heart.

She grabbed one of the spears and went on the attack.

It was frightening to behold.

"Now look at this one," Alice said. She pressed one of the tabs at the bottom and brought up a different clip. Same young Asian woman, now running through a forest of smooth bright green stalks with thin branches way at the top.

Marnie never would have escaped to a forest like that. Not nearly enough cover. She needed heavy foliage, and not so high up. Somewhere she could hide.

The young woman had the same problem. The men chasing her could see her. This was all in ancient times again, it looked like, so they had swords instead of guns. The young woman had no weapon of her own. Marnie's heart was racing hard.

"Watch," said Alice, riveted to the screen.

As the men caught up to her, the young woman grabbed onto one of the thick green stalks and hoisted her body sideways into the air. She kicked out with both feet, hitting one after another in the head. Men fell all around her.

"See, I thought you might like something like that," said Alice. "Keep your arms free, but learn to use your legs."

Marnie couldn't sit any longer. Her heart was running away. She bolted to her feet and started running toward the front of the hangar. She heard Alice calling her name.

Marnie flapped her arms. Took flight. Kept flying out the open doorway.

Into bright sunlight, then curve to her right, back into the shadows of her own hangar.

She flew and flew. Hard. Like a swimmer doing sprints. Freestyle, kicking her feet hard behind her. All the way to the back, flip, swim hard again to the front.

Alice waited below. Worried, Marnie could see. But this wasn't the time to talk. She needed to keep flying. Flying hard.

Her pulse was still wildly out of control. *Why?* She had been able to watch Alice doing *kata*, and it didn't make her feel like this.

It was the aggression. The aggression of the men and of the young woman in response. Too real. Too much violence. Real swords. Real spears.

And what if those had been guns?

The woman had no place to hide.

It was a movie, it wasn't real, but Marnie's heart didn't know the difference. She flew back and forth six more times before she could convince herself she was all right.

She felt tired. Thirsty. And Alice sat just inside the hangar, propped up against the wall, waiting.

Marnie wasn't sure whether to feel comforted by that or annoyed.

She landed softly on top of one of the planes and hopped from there to the ground.

She walked slowly over to Alice. Then sat down beside her against the wall.

"Obviously I did something wrong," said Alice.

Marnie shrugged. For some reason she felt like crying.

"Will you tell me what it is?" Alice asked.

Marnie swiped away a tear that had managed to fall. "You wouldn't understand." She still wasn't sure she did herself.

Alice handed her a bottle of water. Marnie gratefully accepted. Sometimes she forgot to drink until she was so thirsty her mouth and throat ached.

"But it was the movies," Alice said.

Marnie nodded.

"I'm sorry," said Alice. "I thought you'd like them. My mother and I always did."

"Why?" Marnie asked.

"Because we liked to see the possibilities. She was a really good fighter."

"Your mother?"

Alice nodded. "Better than I am."

Marnie didn't miss the *"was."* But she didn't want to ask. She drank the rest of the water, then leaned back against the wall.

"Your boss," she said. "I know what he wants from me. He wants to use me for some military mission or some secret… whatever he does."

"Ted?" Alice asked.

Marnie nodded.

"I don't even know what he does," Alice said. "I just met him two days ago. Believe me, I'm as lost as you are right now. I don't know why he brought me here. I think it was for you, but I'm not really clear."

"To train me in martial arts," said Marnie.

"Probably," Alice agreed. "But not for some mission. He never said anything about that. He told me you were afraid. He asked me to teach you how to be safe. That's all."

Marnie closed her eyes. She could feel the tears coming again. She wished she could believe it was true. That anyone cared about her. Just for her, not for what she could do.

Even her mother had stopped loving her that way.

"Look," Alice said. "I know. You don't know me. You have no reason to trust me. But I'm here. I'm a resource. Use me or don't. I have to be here anyway for however long, and I'm happy to teach you if you want. I've taught a lot of women. I've always thought it was important."

She pushed off from the wall and stood. "I'm sorry if I scared you with those movies. You're under no pressure from me. I have my own work to do. I should get back to it."

She paused in the doorway of the hangar. "I'll have them leave the trampoline. Use it as much as you want. You were really good at it. I think it can help. See you later."

Then she left.

Marnie stayed, overcome with tiredness.

She needed to rest. Sleep, even. Especially if she was still leaving tonight.

She was still leaving.

Wasn't she?

10

Alice worked for another hour or so, but her mind wasn't on it. She gave up and shut off her laptop and walked alone to the mess hall. She ate an early dinner of teriyaki vegetables and rice. Dessert was cheesecake. She ate that too.

She didn't see anyone she knew. Just as well. She needed to look through more files.

None of the day felt like a particular success. She hadn't found any photos of her second attacker. She still had no idea who he was or who he might work for. Why he needed to kill her.

She had practiced *katas*. That was probably fine. She had taught Marnie the trampoline. Maybe that was good. Everything else? A waste.

She unlocked her door and stepped back inside her room. Her laptop sat waiting on top of the desk. Maybe Gina and the other investigators on Alice's case were looking through files of their own. Maybe they had answers already, and someone would get word to Alice soon. Then she could go home again, back to San Diego, back to her job and her well-organized life.

Or maybe no one was working on it, and so it was still going to be up to Alice. To find answers. To dig deeper. To protect herself from whatever this new threat was.

So it made sense that she should boot up again and put in as many hours as she could before she fell asleep.

But something inside her resisted.

She didn't want to.

She wasn't in the mood for more failure. Her mind needed a break.

She could go back to the Hub, get another movie viewer. Watch a few films back to back and let her brain take a vacation.

But that required effort. Going back outside. Walking. And right now all she wanted to do was sit.

It wasn't like her, this lethargy. But she didn't have the will to fight it.

So she lay on top of her scratchy military bedspread and stared up at the ceiling.

Her pillow made a crinkling sound. The comics were still under there where she had hidden them.

Maybe Gina was right. No more work after hours. Just reading fantasy books and comics.

Alice sighed and pulled them out. Thumbed through the first issue. There were five of them, all looking equally ridiculous.

But the cover on the last comic was intriguing. How

did that warrior woman get her wings? Why did Gina think those comics might be useful?

Research, Alice remembered her saying. *Sure.*

She started reading them in order. No point in skipping ahead in the plot. These weren't thousand-page novels, they were just short comics with lots of pictures.

The story began in ancient Rome. The woman warrior, Lenna, was the secret daughter of the goddess Diana.

She grew up with an overwhelming sense of needing to right all wrongs. To protect the innocent. To risk her own life if it meant defeating evil.

But even in the worst fight at the end of the first issue, Lenna miraculously survived.

Surprise, she was immortal, just like her mother.

Well that helps.

She went on to the second comic.

Lenna in medieval times, fighting for what was right. Then Lenna in World War I and World War II.

Next issue.

Alice followed the adventures of Lenna all the way up to present day, then beyond that, into the future.

By the end of the fourth issue, Lenna's enemy had finally discovered how to kill her. Immortals really weren't, if you knew the secret spell.

Lenna died. All was lost.

But then look! The fifth and final installment. Alice could barely force herself to read on. She loved fantasy movies, including superhero ones, but this plot was nowhere as good.

She wondered again at Gina's taste. The investigator seemed to take her job seriously, but maybe Alice had misjudged her overall. Maybe it was right that Alice did her own investigation and didn't rely on Gina to uncover the truth. Maybe Gina wasn't as sharp as Alice thought.

In the final issue Lenna passed over into light and shadow and emerged an avenging angel with wings.

That explained the image on the cover of the comic. Large, impressive wings made of blue and black feathers, Lenna's hands still free to hold her signature sword.

Okay, but here was something. Alice sat up in bed.

Not only did Lenna use her sword, she also attacked with her wings.

Cut, sliced, pierced with the sharp pointing ends of her feathers.

Alice remembered her mother coming home from the hospital once with the story of how a duck hunter had ended up in the emergency room. His arm had been sliced repeatedly all the way to the bone. He had lost an impressive amount of blood.

The duck he shot wasn't quite dead. When the hunter tried to pick it up, the duck fought back. It frantically flapped its wings, and the sharp bones beneath the feathers cut into the hunter's arm. The wings sliced and sliced deeper until the hunter finally had the sense to let go.

It took more than twenty stitches to fix him. Alice's mother always had strange stories like that.

So it wasn't implausible that Lenna could use her

wings as additional weapons. Like knives fanning out from fingers.

Alice thought about that. Looked at the pictures. Considered.

Lenna also wore spike-toed boots to do even more damage.

Could Marnie fly with weight like that on her feet? Alice wasn't sure. But maybe her arms could handle it. Blades on the tips of her fingers.

Alice closed the comic. Was that why Gina wanted her to read it?

Or was it just the concept in general of a woman who was able to fly?

None of this felt like real life. Just a few days ago Alice's concerns were completely different. Guns and knives and assassins, not helping Marnie improve her takeoff and figure out how to fight from the air.

But she couldn't deny it was interesting. Both her parents would have loved it.

Alice glanced once more at her laptop.

She owed it to Aurora and Will Kern to work as hard as she could every single day to uncover the truth behind their killing.

But she knew she wasn't at her best anymore. The day was shot. Her mind felt completely used up. It would be better to go to bed early and wake up fresh and ready to go. Return to her real work in the morning.

Train Marnie in her spare time if Marnie wanted it, but if she didn't, keep all that time for more research.

Satisfied that she had a plan, Alice took a long hot

shower and put on a T-shirt and a clean pair of sweats. Whoever had thrown her clothes in a bag hadn't added any pajamas.

Could Marnie fly with a knife strapped to her hand?

Considering how she'd reacted to the fight scenes, would she ever want to?

11

Marnie kept close to the compound for her night flights. She didn't need to go far. It was like anyone else waking up in the middle of the night to get a drink of water or use the bathroom. Just a slight interruption in her sleep, ten minutes was all it took to calm the urge, and then she could go back to her bed and snuggle under the covers.

It was around two o'clock in the morning. The sky was clear and there was most of a moon.

Marnie circled above the houses. Lights were on in only one of them. Someone who couldn't sleep, or maybe had an early shift. She didn't know how it worked here.

She didn't care.

But she was staying. For now. She thought about it after Alice left that afternoon. Marnie flew and thought about everything Alice said.

And about the reasons Marnie had for wanting to leave tonight.

Those reasons weren't true. She thought they had nets. She thought they would try to capture her. She was wrong. The nets belonged to the trampoline. No one was trying to hurt her. She had to admit to herself she'd misunderstood.

Not that she wasn't still right. Even if Alice didn't know what Ted Whitling had in mind—and Marnie believed Alice was telling the truth about that—Marnie still knew that Ted wanted more from her than just to provide some safe haven where she could fly all day long for free.

The world didn't work that way. She wasn't a child.

Marnie circled the houses one more time, then turned back toward her own building. The night air felt chilly. She had underdressed. She needed to start wearing a heavier jacket. And probably thicker leggings and socks.

Down below, on the path between the offices and Marnie's building, she saw someone walking. A man.

He wasn't rushing, but he wasn't ambling either. His hands were in the pockets of his coat.

He wasn't Ted Whitling. This man was tall and thin. A completely different face.

Marnie didn't know him.

He passed the first group of rooms and continued walking to the second, where both Marnie and Alice were staying.

The man paused. Looked around. Took a few more steps, then stopped in front of Alice's door.

Marnie's pulse shot up. *This is wrong. Something's wrong.*

Her skin felt cold. She swam lower to get a better look.

The man pulled something out of his right pocket.

A gun. Marnie could see it, the shape of it, the way he held it, no question that was a gun.

Marnie's breath felt strangled.

The man reached into his other pocket. Pulled out a set of keys.

Hesitated a moment, searching for the right one. Then he fitted it into the lock.

Marnie only had a second.

She had nothing else. Nothing in her hands, nothing she could throw. She could shout, but then he would see her. He would shoot her instead.

She had nothing but herself.

That had to be good enough.

Marnie clamped her arms to her sides and pointed herself like an arrow.

Feet first, plunging to the earth.

She fell hard on top of the man, knocking him to the ground. Skinny as she was, it was still a hundred and ten pounds falling on his head from the sky.

"Alice! Alice! ALICE!" she screamed.

Alice appeared in the doorway. Marnie saw her kick. Kick the man on the ground in the face, kick the gun from his hand.

Marnie was already running. *RUN! GO!* Flapping her

arms, off the ground, into the air, up where it was safe again.

She was gasping, gulping for air. Her heart battered against her ribs.

She could have been hurt. She could have been killed.

Alice was shouting for help. She held the gun now and pointed it at the man. He still lay flat. He hadn't moved.

Doors were opening all along the row. Lights went on. People were running to see.

Alice looked up into the sky. Marnie saw her. Alice lifted a hand.

Marnie flew on.

But she knew it. *Knew it.* She had just saved Alice's life.

All by herself. She did something.

Tears streamed down Marnie's face.

She didn't want this. She felt terrified. Her heart pounded in her chest.

But she was crying because it worked. She had done something and it worked. She had saved somebody. She did it.

Finally, after all this time.

She thought of the canyon. And her mother.

How she must have felt when Marnie couldn't help her.

How she must have felt when she realized she was going to die.

Marnie sobbed. She flew through the cold night air.

Up higher where she couldn't see, couldn't hear what was going on below.

Maybe she should keep flying forever.
Maybe that was best.
But she had at least done this much. Saved Alice.
Maybe that was enough.

12

Alice sat cross-legged on her bed gripping a cup of coffee. She had wrapped herself in a blanket. The room felt uncommonly cold.

It was four in the morning. Dark outside. Ted Whitling sat on the metal chair that went with her metal desk.

Alice told him everything. At least everything she saw. There were so many details neither of them knew. The security cameras had been disabled.

A third man dead. This time not by her.

Neck snapped by the weight of something heavy falling on his head.

Alice thought she knew what. She just didn't know how Marnie did it.

"His name is Runcon," sad Ted. "He's worked maintenance here the last two years."

"Two years?" Alice felt sick. "Was he embedded or

turned?"

"We don't know," said Ted. "Obviously it's a concern. There are a lot of secrets here we'd prefer not to get out."

Alice thought of Marnie—what someone would think of that secret.

"It's my laptop," said Alice. "How stupid of me to keep using it."

"Could be your account," said Ted. "Logging in to the Agency. It wouldn't matter which computer you used. They'd still find a way to trace you."

Alice set down her cup and wrapped the blanket more tightly around her.

"So now what?" she asked. "I can't ever access the Agency again?"

"We'll give you a ghost account," said Ted. "But for now you have to stop researching whatever files you've been looking at. Obviously that's a trigger."

"But I have to find out!" Alice answered in frustration. "Who's behind this. Who's doing it. How do I know every person I meet isn't the next one they've sent to kill me?"

"We're moving you," said Ted. "Someplace more secure. We'll take care of you, Alice."

Alice groaned. She got up from the bed, still wrapped inside her blanket. She hated having no control.

Her coffee was cold. She filled up the brewer with water from her bathroom faucet and made a fresh cup.

"You're not the only analyst," Ted reminded her. "We have a lot of people at the Agency with a lot more experience than you. Let them do their job."

"And what do I do in the meantime?" she asked. "Just keep hiding and doing nothing?"

"Work with Marnie."

"You're moving me."

"We'll move her too," said Ted.

"What makes you think she'll go?" Alice resumed her place on the bed and sipped the scalding coffee. "She doesn't trust any of us. I don't blame her. If she hadn't helped me tonight…"

Alice pinched her fingers against her eyes. She felt strung out. Lack of sleep. Abundance of nerves.

She jumped at the knock on her door.

Ted drew his gun.

"Santos," Santos called. Alice recognized his voice.

Ted opened the door. Six-foot-three Santos seemed to fill what was left of the small room.

"Transport will be ready at first light," he said. "How you doing?" he asked Alice.

"What optics?" she immediately asked. Her voice came out sharp and strained. "You said Ted told you to back off." She looked at Ted. "What optics?"

He looked uncomfortable, but he answered. "Marnie. I didn't want her to see you being protected by somebody else."

Alice tucked her chin into the blanket and didn't say anything more about it. The decision had put her at great risk, but she couldn't argue with the logic. If she was supposed to be some impressive martial artist, here to teach Marnie to defend herself, why would she need her own bodyguard?

On the other hand, it was hard to deny that posting Santos outside her door might have been a deterrent to the latest assassin.

Or maybe he would have tried to kill Santos first.

"Are you coming with me?" Alice asked him.

Santos nodded. At least that was something. Maybe they had all learned their lesson.

Including her. There was no point standing on pride. She felt better knowing someone Santos's size might scare away the next potential killer.

And the way things stood, it seemed like whoever was behind it would keep sending them until she was dead.

Santos left and Ted stood. "Try to get some sleep. I'll have someone come get you around seven."

"Where is she?" Alice asked. "Do you have any idea?"

"Not in her room," said Ted. "She's out there somewhere flying."

13

Alice waited behind the bay of windows inside the Hub. Ted had rustled up a duffel for her somewhere, military canvas and slightly used. She transferred her few belongings out of the garbage bag.

Ted took her laptop. "We'll give you something clean once you get there."

"Get where?" She realized he hadn't said.

"One of our smaller bases. I think it's better if we don't say more."

She couldn't argue. She felt like everyone around her was suspect.

Even Camper, when he joined them a few minutes later to report on what he'd seen.

"Sorry, sir. No sign of her. Sorry, ma'am," he added to Alice.

She noticed he had returned to *ma'am.*

The advantage to a private jet was the schedule was

fairly loose. But Alice understood the urgency. She knew she needed to go.

"Did you check the hangar?" she asked Camper.

"Not me, but one of the other guys. Yes, ma'am."

It was the only place she could think of.

"Take me out there," she told Ted.

He drove her in one of the transport carts. It barely made any noise.

Another quiet jet sped past them on the runway to the right. One of the Snack Packs. Alice wondered if it was new technology. *There are a lot of secrets here we'd prefer not to get out.*

"Wait here," she told Ted when they were still some distance away. She got out of the cart and ran to Marnie's hangar.

Her eyes adjusted to the muted light. She didn't want to call out or scare her, but she knew if she waited long enough Marnie would eventually fly to the front.

If Marnie was even in here.

Ten minutes, fifteen. No sign of the flier overhead.

She could see Ted where she had left him, waiting inside the cart.

She had to go. That was simply a fact.

Reluctantly she left the hangar. Maybe she should write a note. Leave it in Marnie's room. Ask her to come to wherever they were taking Alice. Ted would probably want that. Ted could easily bring her.

If any of them ever saw Marnie again.

What Alice feared, what she thought she knew, was that Marnie would never return.

She had seen Marnie's fear just from watching a few scenes of make-believe movie fights.

How much more frightened did Marnie feel now when she had actually killed a man?

Alice heard a sound. A single thrum from the hangar on the right.

She raced next door.

Looked up, above the trampoline.

Marnie had jumped a single time and now rose straight up into the air. She flapped quickly, like she did at every takeoff, and now treaded the air with her arms.

She locked eyes with Alice.

It was wrong, Marnie thought. All of it. Her condition, her loss, the way all of her mother's dreams had gone so horribly wrong.

Marnie's loneliness. Her fear. No one would want to live this way.

Wrong that Alice had lost her mother too. Marnie could guess that much.

Wrong that a man had sneaked through the darkness to shoot Alice with a gun.

In the dark hours of the morning Marnie had come to rest on a patch of ground at the base of one of the mountains. She felt cold and tired and hungry.

And not like herself at all.

She didn't often think of the things she meant to do. What was the point? This was her life now. She just had to fly and fly and fly.

But she thought of it now, cold and under the moonlight, the girl she had been at sixteen, the things she thought she would do.

Finish high school. Go to college. Study maps. They were her favorite thing.

Have a dog. Have a boyfriend. Get a job. Save up for a car of her own one day.

Such small, insignificant pleasures.

And by a year later, almost all of them out of reach.

She had never had a friend. Not in eleven years. Not a true friend who knew who she was. Her mother was the last one. Marnie had been alone for so long.

She stopped treading the air. Let her feet float gently back to the trampoline.

Alice waited for her by the ladder.

"Thank you," Alice said. And then she hugged Marnie so hard.

The last few pieces seemed to fall away. Layers of armor Marnie had made from sheets of air and covered herself with over time. She cried. She couldn't help it. But she thought that Alice might be crying too.

"Alice?" Ted Whitling called from the doorway.

Alice let go and wiped her eyes.

"Coming." She looked at Marnie. "They're sending me away. Someplace safer. Do you want to come with us?"

A day ago she would have said no.

A day ago she would have run.

A day ago she did run, but she came back in time to help.

It was important to her, saving Alice.

Maybe the most important thing she had ever done.

It meant her life still had some value.

It meant it mattered that Marnie had survived.

"Okay," she said to Alice. "Yes."

Alice smiled and hugged her again.

The jet had plenty of room for the four of them. Alice and Marnie, Ted, and the living statue they introduced as Santos.

Marnie didn't mind him. She liked how quiet and calm he was.

"He's our bodyguard," Alice said. "Just in case we can use an extra hand."

Ted Whitling hadn't said much at all. Marnie preferred it that way.

Now locked into a jet, higher than she ever flew, Marnie gazed at the mountains below.

She could feel the urge rising. To burst out through the door, open her arms, sail on the wind all alone.

Ssh, she told her restless heart. *Look at me. I'm already flying.*

~

ULTRA

"It stands for ultra secure, ultra secret," Ted Whitling explained. He gave both women a smile. "The naming committee worked overtime on this one."

They were in New Mexico now, according to Ted. Somewhere on the southern side.

Alice looked around as she and Marnie Stemple exited the plane.

The temperature was colder than it had been in Nevada, at the facility called the Aviary. Here they might be at higher altitude, or maybe the late-December cold was just naturally colder than it had been a few days before.

She wore jeans and sneakers and a long-sleeved black T-shirt with a black fleece vest over it. She wished she had a warmer coat, but whoever packed her clothes after the shooting in Alice's apartment must not have expected her to leave San Diego.

Alice looked over at Marnie Stemple. The woman was about her own age, twenty-six or slightly older. A few inches taller than Alice's five-foot-two and thinner. The two of them both had brown hair, but Alice wore hers long, pulled back in a thick ponytail, whereas Marnie's was cut short at the base of her neck.

Alice could see now that Marnie was looking anxious. The flight had taken too long. Only a few hours, but Alice knew that was longer than Marnie liked to be cooped up.

So she did Marnie the favor. "I assume she can fly here?" she asked Ted.

"Of course." Ted turned to Marnie. It's protected air space all around," he told her. "Basically a mushroom cloud-shaped bubble above the facility. We'll show you a map later. If you could just fly above where you see the boundaries for now—"

Marnie ran forward several steps, bounded a few steps more, then leapt into the air. She flapped her arms and gained height right away. Alice watched her go.

"Why are we here?" she asked Ted.

"It's the most secure place we have on this side of the country," he said. "I hope you'll be comfortable."

Alice noticed Santos standing close by this time. At the Aviary, Santos had left Alice alone and stayed away the entire time they were there, even though he had been assigned by the Agency to be her bodyguard.

They had all learned their lesson. Another attempt on Alice's life, this time interrupted by Marnie dropping from the sky onto the assassin's head and breaking his neck in the process.

It was the third man who had tried to kill Alice in the past week.

Also the third man dead. Two by Alice, now one in Marnie's column.

It wasn't a competition. Not something Alice wanted in any way. And she knew Marnie didn't want it either.

If six-foot-three Santos could act as a deterrent, then Alice welcomed the quiet man. He could follow her around all day.

"Will I have computer access?" Alice asked.

"That's..." Ted looked up to watch Marnie's progress across the sky. She had just reached the invisible boundary above the visible fencing around the facility, and turned around to fly back toward them.

"...something we're still working on," Ted finished.

"You promised," Alice said.

"We'll sort it out," said Ted. "I do promise."

He gestured toward the large white building in front of them. "Why don't you get settled? We've put you and Marnie next to each other. Help her get settled too, if you don't mind."

Ted started for the white building, but Alice caught his arm.

"How do I know it's safe this time?" she asked. She was feeling anxious herself. She had never been someone's target before. One attempt on her life had been extreme. But three...

Ted looked her in the eyes. "It's safe. You'll see when I show you around."

"The last one was an insider," Alice pointed out. "It was personnel, not the facility."

"Ultra is different," said Ted. "You'll see."

Alice let go of him. What else could he say? Apart from locking her in a cell somewhere and never letting anyone near her, ever, what exactly could they do?

More than living inside this bubble, she needed the threat itself to go away.

"I need to work on this," Alice said. "I need access."

"Other analysts—"

"I know," she interrupted. "I know." Ted was several inches taller than she was, but she had no trouble standing up to him. He wasn't her supervisor, he wasn't her peer. She still wasn't sure exactly where he fit into the Agency's hierarchy.

"Other people are working on this too," she went on. "You've said. But no one is ever going to care about my life as much as I do. So I need to work on my own case too. Please."

"You're right," said Ted. "Absolutely. I'll try to speed up the process."

Alice gave him a nod, then started for the white building.

Santos flanked her as she moved.

That felt good.

2

Marnie flew from one end of the airspace to the other, then the width, then the length again.

Then four more times. A cross pattern, up, down, side to side.

What am I doing here?

In the moment, when Alice asked her if Marnie wanted to come with her, away from the Aviary with its wide open spaces and mountains to fly over and a tall airplane hangar where Marnie could fly indoors all day long, Marnie had said yes, I'll leave.

Why?

I made a friend.

Garbage. It was a childish, foolish reason.

You invited me to your party! You like me!

Nothing had changed. It was still the feds behind all of this. Taking possession of Marnie like a piece of equipment for them to use.

"Don't you want to serve your country, Ms. Stemple?"

No. What Marnie wanted was to be left alone.

To fly. To live wherever she wanted. To work a job. To live alone.

Liar.

Okay, to fly.

The other things didn't matter.

Having a friend matters.

Alice was temporary. Marnie knew that. There at the Aviary for protection. When that didn't work—

When you killed that man—

Marnie pumped her arms harder.

She thought about it. Too much. The chain of decisions she made one by one, and quickly.

Seeing the man steal through the darkness toward Alice's room. The gun. The key in his hand, turning her lock. The gun.

She didn't regret it.

That fact weighed on her.

Savior complex.

Maybe.

You can't make up for the past.

Marnie saw the fence down below and turned.

She swam through the sky, the freestyle crawl and butterfly.

She could see people down below looking up. Seeing her.

Ever since her first few days back at the Aviary, she didn't worry about that anymore. Ted said there were other people with powers, gifts—what Marnie thought of as her *condition*—and that those people were kept secret too.

So let them look. As long as they didn't bother her. She was just so relieved to fly.

Out in the open, for long, long stretches of time. Not just ten minutes every hour, the way she'd been living for years.

Like trying to breathe through a straw.

Now finally taking these big full lungfuls. She would do it as long as she could.

Let them look. And if anyone did try to bother her, she would run again. Escape. Go where no one knew her. Change her name. Do all of it again. She'd already done it a hundred times in the last eleven and a half years.

She looked down again and saw Alice this time. Along with Santos.

Alice shielded her eyes. She gestured for Marnie to come down.

When Marnie didn't react, didn't shift her flight path to aim for the ground, Alice held up a bottle of water in one hand and a bag of chips in the other.

Marnie smiled.

Alice got her.

3

The rooms at Ultra were better than at the Aviary, Alice noticed. Larger, newer, a little fancier.

"What do you think?" she asked as she showed Marnie to her own room.

Marnie looked around and nodded. "Yeah, it's nice."

It was more of a hotel suite instead of a standard room. There was a couch in the front area, with a coffee table and deep-cushioned upholstered chair nearby. Across from the couch, a desk and chair. All of it was the same in Alice's room.

A counter across from the bathroom with a small sink, mini-fridge, and microwave. Next to the sink a big wooden bowl of fruit. Alice had already snagged a banana from her own bowl.

Past the bathroom, a separate door leading to a bedroom with a king bed, ample dresser, and wall-mounted TV.

It was the kind of place you could settle in and live for a while. If you had to.

Alice wasn't sure how long she would have to.

Marnie tested some of the features. She turned the faucet to the little sink on and off. Opened the refrigerator door and closed it. Same with the microwave.

She looked inside the bathroom. Flushed the toilet. Turned the shower on and off.

When she came back out she saw Alice watching her with a curious look. Marnie shrugged. "I've lived a lot of places. I like to check."

"Look in your dresser," Alice said. "They probably left you some clothes. They left me a whole bunch."

It had been strange to see. Underwear, sports bras, plain T-shirts, fleece sweaters, workout clothes, fleece-lined pants, a hoodie, a warm coat—all in Alice's specifically petite size.

It was like having a personal shopper. Strange, but not necessarily bad. Ted Whitling must have called ahead, asked someone to outfit her. These people worked fast. Alice didn't even know she'd be moving to Ultra until early this morning.

Marnie stood at the dresser now, surveying her wares. She pulled out several of the outfits.

They were different than what was in Alice's room. A few bodysuits made from a thin synthetic fabric. Long john pants and tops. Body-hugging top layers: synthetic sweaters, hoodies, and jackets.

The kinds of things you might want to wear if you were flying out in the open in winter.

Marnie ran her fingers over the cloth. "I've never seen anything like these."

Alice joined her at the dresser. Both of them examined all the clothes.

Marnie rubbed one of the bodysuits against her cheek. "I like it. It's soft."

She took it into the bathroom and shut the door.

Alice called to her through the wood.

"I'm heading over for lunch. Do you want anything?"

Ted had taken her by Cafeteria A, the one closest to Alice's and Marnie's rooms, as part of his initial tour. It was small, about the size of an upscale coffee shop, with five or six tables set up. A few people were in there eating and talking. It was close to lunch.

The place smelled delicious. Alice read the hand-written menu propped on an easel just inside the door: mac and cheese, three different kinds of soup, sandwiches made to order, and lasagna. At the far end of the room she could see a small salad bar.

"When's the last time you ate?" Ted asked her.

She had to think. "Dinner. Last night."

No wonder she felt so empty. She glanced aside at Santos. He seemed hypnotized by the menu. A guy that size probably needed to eat every hour.

Alice had grabbed water and a bag of chips for Marnie, promising Santos they'd come back for lunch soon.

She didn't want to abandon Marnie. This place was new to her too.

Now Santos stood outside between the doors to

Alice's and Marnie's room. Alice needed to keep her promise to him.

Marnie came out of the bathroom. Smiling.

She ran her hands down the smooth fabric of the light gray bodysuit where it hugged her thighs.

"It's like water," she said. "Warm like bath water."

Alice reached over to test the fabric against Marnie's forearms. She tried a few times to lift the sleeve off Marnie's skin, but could never get a grip.

"But it doesn't feel tight," Marnie said. "It feels soft and comfortable. Are you sure they didn't give you one too?"

"Pretty sure," Alice said.

And she was glad of that. Glad that Marnie had something all her own.

She couldn't help feeling sorry for her. Every new piece of information gave her more of a glimpse into what seemed like a lonely life. *I've lived a lot of places.* Alice wondered how many. And was Marnie always alone? Did she have family? Friends?

No one Marnie had ever talked about so far.

Alice jutted her thumb toward the front door. "Santos and I are going for lunch. Do you want to come with us?"

Marnie gestured toward her new flight suit and gave Alice an *Are you kidding?* look. "I'm flying. I'll see you later."

"Oh, here," Alice said, digging the map out of the pocket of her vest. "I wanted to show you."

She spread the map out on the counter.

"It's all restricted airspace above here," she said, tracing with her finger the area of the map where Ted said it would be safe to fly. "Anyone coming in needs permission. Otherwise no one's allowed within miles. No one will track you. You can fly as much as you want."

Marnie nodded. She flicked her fingers against her opposite palm. Alice could feel the impatience pouring off her. She was keeping Marnie on the ground.

But then something on the map caught Marnie's eye.

"There are mountains," she said, pointing.

"Yes, but… too far outside the boundary," Alice said. "Sorry."

She could see the disappointment on Marnie's face.

"But Ted said there's another big hangar here," she quickly added. "He'll have them clear it out so you can fly in there if you want. And he's already ordered another trampoline. It should be here tomorrow."

Marnie nodded.

Alice could still see her disappointment.

Did I do the right thing?

She had been wondering it ever since they landed.

If the security was better at Ultra, then being here was an upgrade for Alice.

But it wasn't for Marnie.

So much less room to fly.

Not the wide open vistas of the mountains near the Aviary.

Restrictions. Limits. It wasn't really fair.

Marnie had saved her life. Alice owed her everything.

"Look," Alice said. "I have to be here right now, but you don't. No one's after you. If you don't like it here, I'm sure Ted will take you back—"

"No," Marnie answered immediately. She let out a breath and smiled. "No, it's fine. And this—" She ran her hand down one of her sleeves. "—might be worth it."

She pulled the tight-fitting hood of the body suit over her head. She tucked her hair in, like a swim cap.

Then Marnie trotted toward the door. Alice followed.

Santos glanced at them as they came out.

Marnie stepped onto the patch of brown grass in front of the rooms, past where the roof overhung.

She bent her knees. Flapped. Jumped straight up.

Flapped hard to keep above ground.

She still wasn't strong enough, Alice could see. Her legs didn't give her enough spring.

Marnie resorted to her regular takeoff, running forward and flapping and ascending on the diagonal.

Alice and Santos watched her gain height.

The flight suit was an interesting thing.

When Marnie first pulled it from the drawer, it looked matte black. Plain.

When Marnie came out of the bathroom wearing it, Alice realized it was actually light gray, with darker strips of gray woven in.

But now it was as blue as the sky.

With patches of yellow and white like the sun reflecting off the surface of Marnie's back.

"Camouflage," said Santos.

An instant later, Alice couldn't see Marnie at all. Not even her face, which a moment before had looked suspended against the blue backdrop.

The bodysuit had made her invisible.

4

F ritz Zimholt watched the video feed.

He was tall, with the upright bearing of a military man. Air Force. It had been his honor and his privilege.

He had worked with all of the branches of the military by now, and with many different aspects of the American government.

Also his privilege. And a duty he had felt since childhood.

Fritz was seventy-four now, mostly bald with a rim of white hair below his temples.

He watched Marnie's takeoff. But what concerned him was the suit.

What *delighted* him, was the suit.

He had used its chemical components in other applications, but never in a fabric.

Other scientists had tried. But their materials

degraded, whether quickly or over time, and Fritz knew he could do better.

Had fought for the chance to do better.

He was known for metals. Airplane parts, oil rig components, combat vehicles, other equipment. Over a hundred inventions patented under his name. He made a good living from his busy mind.

But rumor had reached him.

He quickly went to work.

A young woman who could fly. No external aids, just on her own power, arms pulling her along through the sky.

What does she need?

The question sprang to Fritz's mind, the first question that had led to every invention since he was a teenager. *What do I need? What do my parents... my teacher... a soldier... a mechanic... a pilot... navigator... spy...*

What does that person need?

Insulation, Fritz thought when he thought of the young woman. Warmth in cold weather, cooling in the heat.

Mobility. Nothing too tight or constricting.

Comfort. Nothing in the clothes that would pinch or scratch and distract her over the course of a long flight.

Protection. From the kinds of attacks she might face.

Secrecy.

From what he had learned, it was a fluke that the girl had been brought in. She had evaded notice for several years. That meant she was already good at deception. She had managed to keep her skill hidden despite the world of nosy, curious people.

Fritz Zimholt intended to help her continue.

There were chemical processes he had used in the past to make large very visible objects blend into their surroundings.

Military planes in particular.

If he could translate that formula into a pliable material like fabric, maybe he could do the same for Marnie Stemple.

He set aside all other projects at his private factory and had his designers and engineers work exclusively on the clothes.

From what Fritz had heard, Marnie Stemple was being housed at the Aviary for the time being, but there was a risk she might decide to leave any day. Those who were tasked with trying to convince her to join the effort had not yet closed the deal.

For now he had a window of time, Fritz's informant told him. A window would have to be enough.

Two weeks later, two weeks of constant labor and testing and reworking, Fritz thought he might have succeeded.

But he couldn't be certain. He needed Marnie herself to test it.

On the morning he intended to travel to the Aviary and bring her all the clothes, Fritz learned that Marnie had been unexpectedly transferred to Ultra.

So he changed his plans as well.

He flew directly to New Mexico. Arrived shortly before Marnie and her companions. He gave the various garments to the base commander, who then made sure they were placed in Marnie's room.

Fritz had been watching the video feed of the area outside her room for the past few hours, waiting and hoping that at some point she would emerge wearing the suit.

Finally he watched her go into her room with the short young brown-skinned woman he knew to be Alice Kern.

The fact that Marnie was traveling with Alice was another interesting piece of the puzzle.

Fritz didn't believe in coincidence.

He watched the large security agent, Santos Rodriguez, position himself outside the door. Then Fritz waited.

Finally the door opened again and Marnie ran outside wearing one of the suits.

Fritz stared hard at the screen.

Watched her takeoff, not so good at first, then from a running start she was gone.

Fritz shifted his gaze to the next camera feed. At Fritz's request, the base commander had tasked several of the onsite cameras to aim at various angles into the sky.

Fritz watched Marnie fly.

And in a moment when he should still be watching her fly, suddenly she was gone.

Fritz Zimholt smiled.

He looked at all the screens, searching for her.
Marnie Stemple had vanished.
Exactly as Fritz intended.

5

The air slid over Marnie's head and body. She could feel the pressure of it as she soared through it, but the temperature barely touched her.

The sleeves of the body suit had thumb holes so she could pull them all the way over her knuckles and keep her hands warm.

The leggings didn't stop at her ankles, but encased her whole feet. There was some kind of tougher surface on the bottom, but it was still as light and fluid as the rest of the suit.

The hood kept her hair off her face. Maybe she could finally grow it out instead of always trimming it every few weeks to make sure nothing could blow across her eyes.

At the same time, she never cut her hair so short that it made a statement. Drew attention. It needed to look boring, same, day after day.

She admired how long and thick Alice grew her hair.

Marnie used to have long hair too, when she was younger. She missed it. But after just a few times of flying with it, even tied back in a ponytail or braided, she realized it wasn't practical anymore.

Her mother cut it for her the first time. Even though Marnie asked for it, she still cried. She was sixteen then and cared about how she looked.

Her mother had kissed the top of her head. "You're still beautiful. You're always beautiful."

It was her mother who was beautiful. Tan skin, deep blue eyes, a smile that drew people in, made them want to talk to her, to know her.

Just six months after that haircut, her mother had changed so much Marnie sometimes had difficulty looking at her. Her haggard face, her leathery skin, body reduced to bones. She never smiled anymore. Never laughed. Her blue eyes were still bright, but with a kind of manic energy Marnie couldn't help her manage anymore.

Stop it.

Marnie flattened her arms to her sides and dove fast through the cold air to chase the memories from her mind.

But the joy of flying was over for now. Even the bodysuit wasn't enough.

Marnie turned at the edge of the restricted air space and swam slowly back toward her room.

6

Alice glared at Ted Whitling in frustration.

He didn't appear to care.

Alice had hunted him down, asking multiple people where they thought she could find him. Finally she cornered him in a small windowless office in the middle of one of the nondescript white brick buildings clustered in the middle of the base.

"You promised," Alice said.

"Wasn't my call," said Ted. "Face it, that's how they've tracked you before. If we're going to keep you safe…"

Alice didn't like it. One bit.

No computer access. None. Not even to work on her regular caseload.

Every hour she was wasting time. Work was all she had anymore.

"You're our guest for now," said Ted. "Treat it like paid time off."

"That would be great," Alice said, barely hiding her contempt, "except someone is trying to kill me and I have no way of finding out who it is. "

"Train Marnie," said Ted.

"She doesn't want training."

"She needs it," Ted said.

Alice paused for a moment. Then sighed.

The fact was, Ted was right.

Marnie was vulnerable. Alice knew it.

Even killing a man didn't change that.

Alice could see it in her mind's eye: Someone grabbing Marnie's leg as she took off. Pulling her to the ground and hurting her. Killing her.

Or Marnie doing what she did the night before, diving feet first from the sky and surprising someone on the ground.

But what if it wasn't a surprise? What if someone looked up, and Marnie was already committed, and it was too late for her to reverse course, gain height again and get away?

What if that person had a gun? Thin as she was, Marnie was still a large enough target that someone could get lucky and shoot her.

Every scenario Alice had run through her head since meeting Marnie a few days ago ended up with Marnie dead.

Was Alice really going to do nothing about that?

When the only reason she was alive to argue with Ted right now was because Marnie had saved her life the night before?

Alice sank into the chair on the other side of Ted's desk.

"I don't know how to convince her," she said.

"Gain her trust."

"I think I have her trust," Alice said, "but that doesn't change how Marnie feels about fighting. She doesn't want it. She told me so."

"She obviously didn't feel that way last night," said Ted. "Have you talked to her about it?"

Alice shrugged. "Barely. I don't want to scare her off."

Ted drummed the desktop with his fingers. He seemed to be considering something.

"There's a man here I want you to meet."

Ted dialed a number on his phone.

"I have Alice Kern here," he said. "Can I bring her by?"

Ted disconnected the call. "Come with me," he told Alice.

"Major Fritz Zimholt," Ted told her on the way over. "He's a materials engineer, retired Air Force. He helped the Agency during the Cold War. He still consults sometimes."

Major Zimholt's office was far plusher than Ted's. Thick beige carpeting, a large dark mahogany desk with a few file folders stacked neatly on top, framed black and white photographs on the walls of people and places Alice didn't recognize. Two large windows looked out onto a neatly landscaped courtyard and to the airfield beyond.

Major Zimholt came around the side of his desk when they entered. Ted made the introductions.

"Miss Kern," said Major Zimholt, looking down at her and smiling. His grip was warm and strong.

He reminded Alice a little of her grandfather on her father's side. The German side. Alice had always looked more like her Filipino mother, but her father was there too: in her round face, her round cheeks, in certain ways she smiled.

Major Zimholt was much taller than Grandpa Peter had been, but the two men shared that same bald round head, the broad nose, the fleshy pouches under their eyes. They even had similar square-looking teeth, even though neither of them wore dentures.

Grandpa Peter had died while Alice was in high school. At the time it felt like such a terrible loss.

But she was grateful for it just a few years later. He didn't have to live to see his beloved son and daughter-in-law murdered.

"Please," said Major Zimholt, gesturing to the small conference table in front of the windows. "Sit."

He pulled out one of the blue fabric chairs for Alice and remained standing until she sat. Old manners, just like her grandfather's too.

Major Zimholt settled in across from her. Ted took the seat between.

"Tell me, Miss Kern—"

"Alice, please."

He inclined his head. "Alice, what do you think of Ultra?"

She thought she could hear a faint trace of a German accent, but she couldn't be sure.

"It's… ni—" she started to say, but Major Zimholt broke in.

"Nothing like the Aviary," he said. "Colder, I've always thought."

Alice assumed he didn't mean the temperature. He

was right, it did feel colder. Quieter. Less activity. Fewer people. Less bustle.

She had a view of the airfield out the window to her left. The runway was empty, silent. No jets rushing by every few minutes the way they did at the Aviary. Alice hadn't seen a single plane fly in or out since she arrived.

Even Cafeteria A where she and Santos ate lunch felt deliberately quiet. The layout—small tables close together in a small space—made it easy to overhear conversations. The people at the other tables compensated by leaning toward one another and keeping their voices low.

Alice and Santos didn't speak at all during lunch. They both concentrated on their food: grilled cheese sandwich and tomato soup for Alice, a heaping plate of lasagna and garlic bread for her bodyguard.

Alice couldn't remember being around someone before who made her so comfortable not making small talk.

"Tell me about your friend," said Major Zimholt. "Miss Stemple."

"Major Zimholt made her suit," Ted said.

"Oh!" Alice leaned forward, excited. Any feeling of formality dropped away. "How did you do it? It's amazing! She just disappeared."

"I'm pleased it worked," said Major Zimholt.

"But... how did you do it?" Alice asked.

"Are you aware of the ganzfeld effect?" said Major Zimholt.

"No," Alice said, "I don't think so."

"It's a problem we pilots have," he said. "Optical illusions created by light and shadow. Things…" He puffed out his fingers. "Vanish. To the eyes. The next thing you know, you've flown your plane into a mountain or the ground."

"Major Zimholt has developed a special coating for our military aircraft," Ted said.

Alice smiled, understanding. "Camouflage."

"Yes," said Major Zimholt. "Precisely."

"I don't think Marnie even knows," Alice said. "She just loved it because it felt so comfortable."

Major Zimholt seemed pleased. "A soldier fights with his body. The more comfortable the body is, the better and longer he fights."

Alice felt uneasy.

Marnie doesn't want to fight.

"Tell me what you know of Ms. Stemple," Major Zimholt asked again.

"Not very much," Alice said. "I only met her a few days ago."

"Yet she killed a man for you last night," said Major Zimholt.

Alice hesitated. Then nodded. It wasn't how she would have phrased it, but she couldn't say it was wrong.

"Yes, well, I would like to meet her," said Major Zimholt. He pushed back his chair and stood. He seemed less like an old man, more like a soldier. A man of action.

Again Alice felt uncomfortable.

She was beginning to see things from Marnie's perspective. *People want things from her.*

"I don't know where she is," Alice said.

"Perhaps still flying," said Major Zimholt. "I would like to see that." He gestured politely toward the door. "If we may."

8

———————————

Alice walked a step or two behind Major Zimholt and Ted. Santos walked a step behind Alice.

She felt like she was moving toward something inevitable. A plan others had envisioned for her without Alice ever agreeing.

Find someone to convince Marnie.

Here's someone.

Bring her.

Convince her of what? Alice still wasn't sure.

Marnie had already shared with Alice her own fears: that they would want her to be a fighter or a courier. Put her to some violent or dangerous use that Marnie had no desire to do.

I just want to help you feel safe, Alice had assured her.

She still meant that.

She still needed to do what she could.

At the edge of the airfield Major Zimholt and Ted came to a stop. Both of them looked to the sky.

Alice looked up too.

Then she backed away from the two of them, far enough to be out of their peripheral vision.

She shook her head. Pretended to lift her ponytail off her neck, but then lifted her hand a little higher and flicked it away from her.

Stay away. Go. She hoped Marnie could see her. Would understand the message.

The group stood for the next ten minutes staring upward.

In that time Alice repeated her gestures twice more.

"Maybe later," Alice said.

Major Zimholt looked disappointed. "Yes," he agreed, "perhaps later."

He turned to Ted. "Would you be so kind as to alert them I'll be leaving soon? I need to fly back before tonight."

Ted pulled out his phone.

"Oh, and can I trouble you for my satchel?" Major Zimholt asked. "I left it in the office."

Alice couldn't be sure, but it seemed like a manufactured errand. She could see that Ted thought so too, by the way he looked from Major Zimholt back to her.

But Ted said, "Yes, of course," and left them nonetheless.

Major Zimholt waited until Ted was several yards away before turning back to Alice. "Would you mind accompanying me back to my plane? There's something I would like to discuss with you."

Alice glanced upward. She couldn't help it. She assumed this would be another pitch for bringing in Marnie.

Major Zimholt saw her look. "About something else," he said. He looked over Alice's head to Santos. "You may come too, but I ask that you allow us some privacy."

Alice briefly locked eyes with Santos. But she was curious now, so she nodded to him.

Major Zimholt set off to their right, past all the office buildings and the housing complex, toward a set of hangars in the distance.

He lengthened his stride. Alice hurried on her shorter legs to catch up.

Major Zimholt kept his voice low. "I knew your grandfather."

"You... did?" It wasn't at all what Alice expected. "How?"

Her grandfather had been a grocer. How would the two of them ever have met?

"Peter was a good man," said Major Zimholt. "Very reliable. Sensible. We served together during the Vietnam war."

Alice remembered some of her grandfather's stories. It wasn't something he spoke of often, but enough that she knew the basics.

"But he was in the Army," she said. "Not Air Force."

"Yes," Major Zimholt agreed.

Alice kept pace with him and waited for more.

She glanced back. Santos walked further behind them than before, but Alice could see that he was alert, watchful. She felt no danger with Major Zimholt, but it was still good to see that Santos hadn't let down his guard.

Major Zimholt's voice was still quiet. "One wonders sometimes what motivates a person. The choices he makes. Loyalty, friendship, honor. A sense of integrity. Peter Kern was a man like that."

Alice's throat suddenly felt thick. The last thing she expected was to hear from a stranger about her grandfather. She agreed with everything Major Zimholt said. That was the man she knew too.

"But there are other kinds," said Major Zimholt, his voice returning to its regular volume. "Men motivated by greed. Or a lust for power. Or simple cruelty. I've seen too many like that."

Alice thought of the man who had gunned down her parents and the rest of the people in the crowd. Cruelty, yes, but she also suspected it was more. Maybe it was greed. Or something else. She had been following the thread for the past year.

Alice continued to walk quickly at the Major's side. Up ahead she could see a row of airplane hangars. There might be ten or twelve. She wondered which one Ted was having cleared so Marnie could fly inside.

In front of the hangars were a variety of small planes, including, she assumed, the jet that had brought them there that morning.

Major Zimholt came to a halt. He looked down at Alice in a grandfatherly way. "I really would like to meet your friend," he said. "Before I go. I want her opinions about the suit. I have some ideas for further modifications, but I would prefer to hear from her."

He seemed sincere. And Alice could understand him wanting to know from Marnie whether his work was a success.

She had no idea if Marnie was still up there in the sky somewhere, still flying. But as between sitting in her room and being up in the air, Alice thought she could make a guess.

She waved her arm. Then both arms. Crooking them toward her. Nodding. All the movements larger than normal, meant to be seen from a distance.

"I know about Danic," said Major Zimholt.

Alice's arms froze.

"Don't react," Major Zimholt said quietly. "Keep gesturing."

Alice's blood felt like ice. But she forced herself to keep moving her arms. She and Major Zimholt stood side by side, both looking up to the sky.

"It's good he's dead," said Major Zimholt. "I know who he worked for."

Alice's heart hammered in her chest. Danic was the beginning of all this. The man who broke into her apartment just four nights ago. Armed. Alice had shot him before he could attack.

"Who?" Alice asked. It felt unreal. To have searched so hard for a name, only to have it dropped into her lap.

"His name is Lavrev," said Major Zimholt in a clear voice. "A very dangerous man."

Lavrev? Alice had never heard the name before. Or seen it in any files.

Why would a stranger want her dead?

What had she uncovered that made her such a threat?

And how was she supposed to defend herself when she didn't know who else was coming for her?

Alice heard movement behind her. Could feel that Santos had moved closer.

Good. Right now she wanted more protection. She felt exposed by how much she didn't know.

Major Zimholt seemed to read her thoughts. "You mustn't trust anyone," he said. "Not even me—"

"Alice, GUN!" Santos shouted.

She jerked to her left, saw Santos aiming his gun.

Not at her. At Major Zimholt.

Alice reacted instinctively. Drove her shoulder into Major Zimholt. Felt him lose his balance before he spun around.

She saw the gun in Major Zimholt's hand. Too slow. Too late.

"NO!" a voice cried.

Santos's hand jolted to the side just as a shot cracked the air.

Then Major Zimholt fired.

And Marnie fell from the sky.

Marnie aimed, kicked, nearly missed, but caught Santos's hand with the edge of her heel.

Her leg continued to sail forward and she lost control. All the strength in her arms was gone. She had been hovering above the group for too long, worried, listening. Hovering was always so much harder than flying. By the time she needed to kick, her arms were shuddering from the strain. She couldn't hold her weight anymore.

She tumbled in front of Santos. Something slammed into her chest.

The force of it spun her to the right. She tried to catch herself, but her ankle gave way, and she hit the ground hard on her side. Her head bounced against the asphalt.

Everything went black.

10

Alice had to wait until it was safe. Then she raced to Marnie's side.

She lifted Marnie's head into her lap. Blood covered the right side of Marnie's face. Alice gently peeled the hood off her head to examine the wound. Marnie's short brown hair was plastered to the sides of her face, wet with sweat and blood.

"Is she all right?" Major Zimholt called.

"I don't know," Alice said, her throat catching. She felt for Marnie's pulse. Steady, but not strong.

She could see Ted in the distance sprinting toward them down the side of the airfield. Behind him a few other people moved into action.

Marnie stirred.

Her eyelids opened a crack.

"I'm here," Alice said, reaching for Marnie's hand.

"Did you get him?" Marnie asked.

"Yes."

"Good." Marnie closed her eyes again.

Ted arrived, chest heaving. He quickly took in the scene: Santos lying dead, Major Zimholt on his knees holding his bleeding arm, Marnie pale and bloody and unconscious in Alice's arms.

"Alive?" Ted asked.

Alice nodded.

Ted's shoulders sagged in relief. He bent over, hands on knees, and caught his breath.

Alice could see one of the base's electric carts racing toward them from the distant buildings.

Ted looked over and saw it too.

"Tell me fast," he said.

Alice had already replayed the scene in her head, trying to understand the sequence.

"Santos yelled that Major Zimholt had a gun," Alice said. "But he didn't. Not then. Santos fired, but I think Marnie kicked his hand. The bullet hit Major Zimholt's arm. Then he shot too, but Marnie fell in front of Santos. I-I think she took the shot."

Alice pointed to Marnie's pale gray suit, just above her collar bone on the right. There was a dark dirty smudge there, but the material was still intact.

Ted looked over at Major Zimholt. "Bulletproof?"

"Theoretically," said Major Zimholt. "I wasn't sure."

Alice laughed. A low burst of a chuckle that surprised herself. But it was her honest and first reaction.

The transport arrived. A long cart with seats in front, cargo space behind. Two uniformed personnel, a man and a woman, grabbed a backboard from the rear of the cart and hurried it over to Marnie.

Alice stood back as they gently loaded Marnie onto the stiff board and secured her with fabric straps. They carried her carefully back to the cart.

"You too, sir," Ted said.

Major Zimholt rose stiffly onto his legs. "No, I can walk. You stay with Marnie. Alice can help me back."

Alice started to protest. She wanted to go with Marnie, make sure she was all right.

But she also knew she and Major Zimholt needed to talk. To sort through everything that had just happened.

And why.

Ted joined the group on the cart and Alice watched it speed away. She glanced finally at the sight she'd been avoiding: her former bodyguard lying dead on the ground. Shot through the neck by Major Zimholt.

They had shared a lunch not so long ago.

She had felt safe having him near. Not so long ago.

She even felt safe for that brief moment when she saw Santos aiming his gun at Major Zimholt, not her. Shouting a warning to her, as if maybe he was going to protect her.

But the lie was already in her ears. "Alice, GUN!" There was no gun. Major Zimholt was no threat.

At least not to her.

"Was it you saying the name Lavrev?" she asked now.

Major Zimholt took a few slow steps until he was at her side. "I believe so, yes," he said. "A gambit on my part. Not a very wise one."

Alice thought about offering her arm to Major Zimholt, but he didn't seem to need it or want it. Even injured, he maintained an upright kind of dignity. She matched his slower pace as the two of them walked toward the cluster of administrative buildings in the distance.

"Who is he?" Alice asked. "Lavrev."

"A favored Russian oligarch, to some. Head of the largest Russian syndicate. But we believe he's even more than that. He has tentacles everywhere. We've been watching him for years."

"But you've never arrested him?" Alice asked.

"He stays in Russia," said Major Zimholt. "Out of our hands. The best we can do is keep cutting off all his associates."

"What about Santos?" Alice asked. "You think he worked for him?"

"Not directly," said Major Zimholt. "But for someone lower in the chain. Like Danic did."

Alice gripped the sides of her arms as she walked along. She felt cold. She wished she had worn one of the thicker jackets someone had left in her dresser drawer, instead of her own black fleece vest. Clouds had moved in, covering the afternoon sun. The temperature might have dropped five or ten degrees in just the last half hour.

Or maybe the shock was starting to wear off.

"Why did you suspect him?" Alice asked.

Major Zimholt gave her a slight smile. Or maybe it was a wince. "I suspect everyone," he said. "You should too. This is a dangerous game we're all playing. I assume you know that by now."

Alice stopped. She looked up at him, frustrated. "I know that people keep trying to kill me. But I still don't know why."

"Don't you?" Major Zimholt checked the state of his makeshift bandage. He readjusted the wad of cloth and continued walking. "You seem an intelligent young woman, Alice. I think you know more than you're saying."

Alice walked in silence for a time. And thought about how much to reveal.

She did know things. Things she had spent the last year tracking and documenting and diagraming, trying to tie one piece of evidence to another. Finding connections. Links. This person to that one, this bank account, that one, those companies, across the country, different cities, different states, a vast network, and she still thought she understood only a fraction…

"Is there anything you want to tell me?" asked Major Zimholt.

Alice did. She longed to share her research with someone after all this time.

And clearly Major Zimholt had information of his own he could share. *Lavrev.*

But she agreed with Major Zimholt's warning.

"You told me not to trust anyone," she said. "Even you."

"Yes," said Major Zimholt. "Although I intended to say more. You shouldn't trust anyone, even me, until you've made your own determination. Don't assume that everyone at the Agency is like you. Some are compromised. It's an unfortunate fact that even our friends can betray us."

"What about Ted Whitling?" Alice asked.

"My opinion?" said Major Zimholt. "A good man. A good agent. Solid. Trustworthy. But that's my opinion, based on my own experience and analysis. I could be wrong. You should decide for yourself."

Alice mulled that over for a moment. "How well does Ted Whitling know you?"

"Better than some."

"What *doesn't* he know about you?" Alice asked.

Major Zimholt smiled. He gave her a look that might have been approval.

"My background," he said. "My reasons."

"Reasons for what?"

"Taking care of this country," said Major Zimholt. "Just as you have reasons. Why did you join the Agency? I understand you originally intended to go to medical school."

Alice stiffened. Briefly. But then she continued walking as before. The information was in her file, no doubt, but the fact that Major Zimholt had bothered to look at it… that surprised her.

Who was she to him? Why would he bother looking up any information about a low-level analyst like her?

Maybe it was because he knew her grandfather. Or maybe it was simply that word had spread in the Agency about a low-level analyst who kept having people try to kill her.

"Will you tell me about Lavrev?" Alice asked. "Everything?"

"Not everything," Major Zimholt answered. "Some of it is beyond your clearance. But I can tell you much of it."

They were at the administrative complex now. Alice didn't know where to go next.

But Major Zimholt clearly did. She followed him to one of the buildings beyond where his office was.

It was plain white, just like the other buildings, with just a letter and number above the door, C-24. Major Zimholt opened the door and held it for her. Alice passed through into the clinic.

Marnie looked like death. Skin so pale she seemed to be drained of any blood. An IV tube jutted from her arm into a bag of clear liquid hanging from a pole on the left side of her bed. Ted sat in a chair on the opposite side, holding her pale hand.

Someone had substituted a hospital gown for her bodysuit. Alice could see a livid bruise blossoming across Marnie's chest where the gown came together in a V.

They had cleaned the blood from Marnie's face, exposing the dark bruise underneath. Butterfly bandages covered some of the cuts on the side of her face.

Ted looked up as they came in. In the short time she had known him, Alice had never seen him look so grave.

A woman doctor wearing blue scrubs turned at the sound of the opening door.

"Major Zimholt," she said. "If you would take the bed over there."

Alice read her ID badge: *Sabbagh MD*. Mid-forties

maybe, short black hair. Dark eyes, light olive skin. Dr. Sabbagh motioned for one of the three nurses in the room to go attend to Major Zimholt. He sat on the edge of the bed and allowed them to peel away the scraps of his sleeve.

Alice moved to Ted's side and crouched beside him. "How is she?"

Ted looked at Dr. Sabbagh, gave her a nod toward Alice. "Go ahead."

"Concussion," the doctor said. "Broken right ankle. Multiple contusions. Severe bruising to her right ribs, leg, and hip. Soft tissue injuries to the right side and upper chest."

Alice felt sick. All her hopes for Marnie were that she would be stronger, safer—not broken. Not broken because of Alice.

But Dr. Sabbagh wasn't finished. "Severely dehydrated," she went on, and Alice thought she detected a note of anger in the doctor's voice. "Undernourished. Underweight. Suffering from exhaustion, I'd say. If she's one of yours, Whitling, I'm surprised you let her get to this state."

Alice and Ted exchanged a look. Alice could see he didn't appreciate the criticism.

But he didn't try to defend himself. Doctor Sabbagh turned abruptly away to tend to Major Zimholt.

Alice wondered what she might have said if the doctor had spoken to her that way instead.

Alice didn't have a good answer to give.

Because Dr. Sabbagh was right. Alice should have seen

what was happening with Marnie. The hours and hours of flight, both here and before, at the Aviary. Barely eating. Barely drinking. The stress of the last twenty-four hours, facing great danger twice.

Protecting Alice twice.

Alice stood. Looked down at Marnie's ghostly pale face once more.

"I need to talk to you," she told Ted. Then she left without waiting for his answer.

She caught Major Zimholt's eye on the way out. He sat stoically while a nurse cleaned his wound and dressed it. Alice avoided looking at Dr. Sabbagh beside him and pushed out through the door.

11

"What are we doing?" Alice asked Ted.

To his credit, he didn't ask what she meant.

He shook his head. Seemed to be having trouble with it himself. He was the one who brought Marnie to the Aviary in the first place. Alice wasn't responsible for that.

"She has to be able to fly," Alice said. "You know that. But now with all the damage…" Her voice caught. She cleared it. This wasn't a time to appear weak.

She needed logic. Facts. She needed to protect Marnie.

Not cry and say how guilty she felt about all of it. That wouldn't do Marnie any good.

"They can sedate her for a few days," Ted said. "Let her get some rest. Maybe some intravenous fluids. Get her to eat."

Alice scoffed. "Okay, that's for a few days. I'm talking about all the rest of it. You have to let her go."

"She's not a prisoner," Ted said. "We have her under

protection…" He held up his hand, warding off Alice's scorn. "I know. But we weren't doing that bad of a job. Before."

"Before *me*," Alice said. It was obvious.

She pivoted away. Paced in the opposite direction, just to stop talking for a minute and think. To stop listening. To try to come up with the best solution.

Any solution at all.

"I keep drawing these people with me," she said. "I'm the one putting Marnie in danger. Let her go back to the Aviary. She was happy there. I'll stay here."

"And then what?" Ted asked. "She just flies all day in a hangar?"

"There are mountains there."

"It's winter," Ted said. "It'll start snowing any day."

"Then take her someplace warm," Alice said.

Ted sighed. "There's a bigger picture here."

Alice rounded on him. "What, that you want to turn her into some spy tool? Or some…" She thought of what Marnie said. "Weapon?"

"No," he said. "Not at all. I promise."

He shifted closer to Alice. "Listen, just *talk* to her, all right? Ask her what *she* wants."

"She doesn't know what she wants," Alice said. "Because she doesn't know why she's here. No one's told her anything. Why haven't you?"

"The truth?" Ted said. "Because we don't know enough. We're still studying her. I just met her myself a little over two weeks ago. Before that nobody knew she existed. It's not like there's some protocol I can follow. This is all new."

Alice blew out a long breath. Ted's answer made sense. Somewhat.

"I heard about you," Ted said. "About how you defended yourself. I heard about your..." He gestured toward her small frame. "Stature. And the truth is, I thought, 'Maybe this is an idea.' Because it's clear Marnie's afraid. Of me, of people, of... I don't know how long her list is. It's how I approach a problem. Chip away at it. Start with the known: afraid. Okay, let's address that. Help build her up. Help build her trust."

Alice sat down on the sidewalk just outside the clinic. All the fight had gone out of her. She couldn't argue with what Ted said. She couldn't argue with anything else at the moment. She needed food. Coffee. Rest. Marnie wasn't the only one who needed better self-care.

Ted's cell phone rang. "Whitling," he answered.

Alice suddenly realized how cold she was. Sitting on the cold concrete didn't help. She dug her hands deep into the pockets of her black fleece vest and wished again she had worn something warmer. The overcast sky chilled her to her bones.

Or maybe it was the shock wearing off.

"Where?" Ted asked into his phone. Alice hunched over to keep warm and listened. "How many?" he said. Then a few moments later a sharp, "Right. Thanks."

Ted ended the call and cursed.

"They found a few artifacts on Santos's body," he said.

"Like what?" The truth was, Alice had forgotten all about Santos. She was more concerned for Marnie.

Ted held out his hand. Alice took it and let him hoist her to her feet.

"We have to talk to the Major," Ted said, reaching for the handle of the door.

Alice grabbed his arm. "Tell me first."

Ted gave a weary sigh. But he let his hand drop.

"Earpiece," he said. "So small you wouldn't see it. Looks like two-way comms. He could hear them, they could hear him."

"Who's *they*?" Alice asked.

"Unknown at the moment."

"But not the Agency?" Alice asked.

"Definitely not," Ted said.

Now it was Alice's turn to curse. She felt a sick swoop in the pit of her gut. It was true then. Santos really had betrayed them.

"How long was he with the Agency?" she asked.

"Long time," Ted said. "Eleven, twelve years."

Alice didn't say it, but she actually felt relieved. Santos hadn't come on board just for her. He was here already, long before she even thought of joining the Agency. While she was still a teenager, living at home. While her parents were still very much alive.

"There was something else on him," Ted said. "They aren't sure all its functions yet. Maybe GPS, camera, live-stream video, they're still looking into it."

"Where was it?" Alice asked.

Ted pointed to his wrist. "Medical bracelet."

Alice remembered seeing it. Noticing it. Deliberately not asking about it. It wasn't her business if Santos had some medical condition he wanted to alert first responders about. The man looked as healthy as she was.

But now a detail nagged at the back of Alice's brain.

Something she had forgotten in the midst of all the commotion.

Why did Marnie kick Santos's hand?

Because it was clear to Alice now that that was what she saw.

Did Marnie know something? Had she seen something?

Santos was there to guard Alice, as far as anyone knew. Why would Marnie try to stop him from doing that?

Why wouldn't she have attacked Major Zimholt instead?

Alice replayed the moment in her head: Santos yelling, "GUN!"

Then another voice—Marnie's—shouting, "NO!"

"She knew," Alice said, as much to herself as to Ted. "Marnie knew Santos was dirty. That's why she tried to stop him."

Now it was Alice who yanked open the door to the clinic.

Marnie's eyes were still closed, but at least some color had started coming back into her face. Alice noticed now that the scrapes on Marnie's cheek from where she landed on the asphalt ended in a neat line just past the edge of her eye where the hood of her bodysuit had protected her face.

She saw Major Zimholt, now with his arm neatly bandaged and cradled in a black padded sling, sitting in the chair next to Marnie's bed that Ted had previously occupied.

Dr. Sabbagh and two of her nurses were in a glass-walled room at the end of the clinic, all three of them typing on their laptops. One nurse remained near Marnie adding notes to a digital chart.

Major Zimholt looked up as Alice burst into the room. She rushed to Marnie's side.

Marnie's eyes remained closed. Alice crouched beside her, mindful of the nurse, and whispered, "Marnie, it's Alice. Can you hear me?"

"She's sedated," Major Zimholt said. "I don't know how deeply."

And there was the concussion, Alice remembered.

She had to wait. There was nothing for it. Even though Marnie might hold some of the missing pieces.

Just like Major Zimholt.

Alice looked at him across the bed.

Should she trust him?

Should she trust anyone anymore?

What was her alternative? To go it alone?

Without any protection or information?

She needed the Agency.

Didn't she?

She stood up again. "I need food," she told Ted wearily. "I can't think anymore right now. And not Cafeteria A," she thought to add. "I don't want to go back there."

What would it feel like to walk in there, knowing she had sat at a table with Santos just a few hours before?

She didn't want to know.

"We're in C," Ted said. "There's one close by. Join us, sir?" he asked Major Zimholt.

Alice wouldn't have invited him on her own. She already wished Ted weren't coming with her. She didn't want to talk to anyone for a while.

Santos was always so good about that.

Maybe because he was always listening for messages coming in on his earpiece.

Alice wasn't ready to think about any of that yet.

A few cups of coffee and a bowl of mushroom risotto later, she returned to the clinic to check on Marnie. Ted had answered another call and abruptly left Alice alone.

The lights in the clinic were muted. Marnie still slept.

Alice sat beside her and laid her hand on top of Marnie's. Her skin felt too cold. But Alice could see Marnie's chest rise and fall with each breath, and the heart monitor she was wired to beeped at a steady pace.

Alice let go of Marnie's hand and slumped forward in the chair. She propped her elbows on her thighs and rested her forehead on her open hand.

"Will you take advice?" a voice asked behind her.

Dr. Sabbagh stood with her hands inside the pockets of her lab coat, still looking as stern as she did before.

"Yes," Alice said, straightening up. Right now she needed as much information as she could get.

"This woman isn't a machine," Dr. Sabbagh said. "Don't let them treat her like one."

Alice looked into the doctor's dark eyes. There was no mistaking the anger there. But also a tinge of worry. Or maybe it was simple compassion.

Alice wondered what else Dr. Sabbagh had seen here at Ultra to make her think she needed to say it.

But Alice didn't ask any questions. She simply nodded.

Dr. Sabbagh turned and walked away.

Alice left the clinic in search of Major Zimholt.

She found him in his office, sitting behind his impressive and tidy desk, his left arm still in its sling. He typed one-handed into a small laptop.

Alice realized a moment too late she had forgotten in her haste to knock.

But Major Zimholt stood politely, just as he did before, and gestured for her to join him at the round conference table near the windows. He still held out one of the blue fabric chairs for her with his one good hand and waited for her to be seated before he took his place across from her.

Old manners, no matter what.

The shades had been drawn. It was fully dark now outside.

But Alice wasn't ready to return to her room just yet.

There would be no protection for her tonight. No Santos posted outside the door. No Marnie flying through the skies.

Protection and safety were only illusions. Even the security alarm in Alice's apartment had only given her enough time to draw her gun before Danic had the chance to kill her.

It had still been up to Alice to protect herself.

She had let down her guard these past few days.

Assumed the Agency would take care of her instead.

She wouldn't make that mistake again.

And if the Agency would no longer provide her with access to the research files…

Did she really need them anymore?

"I want to know everything you can tell me about Lavrev," she said. "Will you tell me now?"

"If you are willing," Major Zimholt answered, "I prefer to show you. But it means leaving Ultra. And deciding whether you trust me."

～

THE CANYON

1

"Merry Christmas," Alice said.

Her voice cut through the haze of sedatives Dr. Sabbagh administered to Marnie every few hours.

To keep the need tamped down. To allow Marnie to heal.

But Marnie felt it, here beneath the pain from her broken ankle and the various cuts and bruises all over her face and body.

The low and insistent thrumming through her nerves every second of every minute of every hour.

Fly. Fly now. GO.

Marnie would have to be unconscious for it to go away.

Or would some part of her still feel it even then?

"Merry Christmas," she answered, smiling. Her voice sounded hoarse. She coughed to clear it.

She had talked a lot yesterday. Once she came out of

the initial and heavier sedation, Ted Whitling was there to question her about everything.

How she knew about Santos.

"I heard him," Marnie said. "I was flying overhead and I saw him go out to the edge of the compound by himself. Then I heard him say my name."

"Calling you?"

"No, talking about me to someone," Marnie said.

"On his phone?"

"Just to the air," Marnie said. "Like he was talking to himself."

"What did he say?" Ted asked.

"That I had a flight suit that made me invisible. And that there wasn't much time. Someone named Major... something was here—"

"Zimholt?"

"Yes," Marnie said. "That. I think so. Then Santos asked whether he should grab me now or still wait."

Her heart raced just at the memory of it. Having to say it out loud.

The dual shocks of learning that the soft, comfortable, wonderful suit she wore made her invisible to everyone else.

And the threat that Santos was supposed to grab her for someone.

Who? Why? Panic flooded Marnie's veins. She wanted to fly away then, fly fast, past the boundary, keep going, never stop. But even if they couldn't see her, could they still track her? The heat of her body. Radar.

She needed to stay where she was for now. Listen. Find out more.

Then tell Alice. Alice would know what to do.

Marnie tried to force herself to be calm. Santos couldn't see her. He said so himself. She had to believe that.

So she hovered above him, her heart pounding, and tried not to make any noise. She felt sure that anyone could hear her ragged and panicked breath.

"Wait a minute," Ted said. He continued rapidly scribbling it all down on a yellow legal pad in handwriting so appalling, Marnie wondered whether he would even be able to read it afterward.

"Go on," he said without looking up.

"I was pretty close to him by then," Marnie said, "but I couldn't really hear any more. Santos just kept saying yes, he understood. He said it a couple of times. Then he stopped talking and walked back toward all the buildings."

"And you followed him," Ted said.

Marnie nodded.

Ted's hand paused above the legal pad. He looked her in the eyes.

"Who drew first? Santos or Major Zimholt?"

So that old man was Major Zimholt.

"Santos," Marnie said. "I tried to kick his gun away, but..."

She could almost feel the impact of the bullet again. The way it slammed into her chest, spun her around.

Then falling to the ground. The pain in her ankle. Pain everywhere, then everything went black.

Marnie could hear the heart monitor beside her start pinging at a rapid rate. Ted Whitling put his hand on top of hers as if to calm her.

Dr. Sabbagh came rushing from her office at the end of the room.

"That's enough," she barked out at Ted.

But the drugs in Marnie's bloodstream were already doing their work. They seemed to sense her distress and immediately began flooding her veins with more.

Marnie could feel a thick and weighty lethargy tugging at her mind. Making her want to sleep. Dragging her back toward a graying darkness despite the morning sunshine she could see streaming through the clinic windows.

She could feel that same weight on her mind now, tempting her to snuggle back down beneath her covers and sleep away the rest of the day.

But it was Christmas. And Alice was here.

Marnie sat up straighter in bed and opened her sleepy eyes wider. She gave her head a slight shake to try to clear it.

"How do you feel?" Alice asked. She sat down carefully on the edge of Marnie's king-sized bed.

"Better," Marnie said.

Alice gave her a skeptical look.

"I am," Marnie assured her. A day and a half had already passed. It had to be true.

Dr. Sabbagh must have thought so too, since she let

Marnie return to her own room at Ultra, rather than spend Christmas Eve and Christmas in the clinic.

She had even let one of the nurses take Marnie out in a wheelchair yesterday for a quick excursion.

Marnie was glad about that now as Alice handed her a wrapped package.

Marnie fished under the pile of pillows beside her to retrieve a gift of her own.

Both boxes were wrapped in the same paper. It was the only kind the little shop at Ultra had. Dark blue background, red and white stars.

More patriotic than festive, but Marnie didn't mind.

It was the first time anyone had given her a Christmas present in years.

She tore into the wrapper. Opened the square box. Inside was a long green plaid scarf and a pair of dark blue fleece gloves.

Also from the same small shop. Marnie had noticed them there yesterday.

"I know you can't fly in the scarf," Alice said, "but I thought maybe the gloves. And you can wear the scarf whenever you're on the ground. I think it's going to get colder."

Marnie smiled shyly. She felt self-conscious. Exposed. Someone buying her something just for her. It wasn't the way things normally were.

"Open yours," she said, deflecting.

Alice opened the wrapping paper neatly where it was taped. Marnie had tried hard to make it look nice. Sharp corners the way her mother had taught her. Not just slapped together the way she sometimes used to wrap her gifts.

It was a stuffed bear. Brown with round ears and dressed in a green sweater with a red pine tree on it. Alice looked surprised, but she had the good manners to act like she liked it. She pressed its soft fabric against her cheek. "I love it," she said. "Thank you."

"Not much selection—"

"I love it," Alice said seriously. "It's been a long time since anyone gave me something like this."

There was something in her expression. Almost a catch in her voice. Marnie thought she might actually mean it.

She looked down at her scarf and gloves. Smoothed her hand over the soft plaid cloth. It smelled new, straight from whatever factory they made it in, and even that felt special in its way.

Alice didn't have to get her anything. They hadn't talked about it or agreed. Yes, it was Christmas, it was traditional, but neither of them had to do it.

It was nice, this way, both of them coming up with the idea themselves. Picking out what they thought the other would like.

Christmas had always been hard for Marnie.

Not always.

For a long time.

Even when she had jobs where there were Christmas parties, she never went.

She flew on Christmas, just like every other day.

But Christmas wasn't every other day. It was the last

normal holiday she ever had with her mother before it all began.

Before Marnie's life broke apart.

A lump caught in her throat.

The heaviness inside her head seemed to drop down to her heart.

There was an ache there. The kind of pain Dr. Sabbagh's drugs could never touch.

Marnie could feel a different kind of urge thrumming through her. Different from the urge to fly.

Maybe it was the drugs sabotaging her normal defenses. Maybe it was all the shocks of the recent days.

Or maybe it was this relative stranger sitting on the side of Marnie's bed, looking at her with concern, seeming to sincerely care about how Marnie felt.

Maybe it was time. Maybe Alice Kern was finally the right person to hear it.

"I think… I might want to tell you something," Marnie said. Her voice sounded so thin and weak to her own ears.

"Okay," Alice said.

Marnie kept her eyes on the green plaid scarf in her hands. She stroked her thumb across the soft cloth. She couldn't look at Alice, not now, not if she was really going to say it.

"About how it happened," Marnie said. "Why I am the way I am."

"Okay," Alice said quietly.

Marnie cleared her throat.

2

My mother was an anthropologist. Dr. Susan Stringer. That's my real last name. Stemple is made up. That's why no one knows who I really am.

My mother was a professor. Very smart. Funny, sweet, a great mom.

It was just the two of us. My biological father wasn't in the picture. The two of them met at a conference and had a one-night stand, and that was me.

We'd lived a few different places, wherever she was teaching. Missoula, Montana for a while when I really little, then University of Idaho later, and when she had a little trouble there we moved to Utah.

She got a job at SUU. Southern Utah University in Cedar City. Close to Cedar Breaks National Park.

There were a lot of beautiful places around there. We'd drive all over. Go camping and hiking. We loved Zion and Bryce and all the canyons all around. The hoodoos and spires and cliffs. My mother used to say it was like living inside a photograph, it was so unreal. Or like someone had painted us into a picture.

She studied ancient civilizations. Not like Greece and Rome, but places in South America and Africa and Asia. She studied artifacts and oral histories and petroglyphs.

Her main field was rituals. She was obsessed with them. Any old and weird thing some tribe used to do, she'd find out everything she could from every source she could find.

We never had much money. She couldn't travel the way she wanted. Some of her colleagues went all over the world looking at archeological digs or visiting museums or talking with other scholars, but my mom had me and she didn't think it was safe to take me any of those places. So she had to research it all from where we were.

We'd go camping somewhere and at night if we could make a fire she'd sit and tell me stories just like we were ancient people and she was a shaman or the storyteller and I was the rest of the tribe.

She wasn't my mom then, she was a leader. My guide. She was telling me things about life and the universe and holy things about the spirit. I could barely breathe sometimes, I was so mesmerized. She was wonderful.

Then on one of our campouts she started telling me a new kind of story.

About how nature is always the same. Societies change, civilizations come and go, but nature—nature is always what it was.

If someone could do something in nature a thousand years ago, nature would let us do that same thing now.

She said it was like being able to see molecules under a microscope. Molecules existed always, but we just couldn't see them until we had the right instruments.

Or like light on a spectrum. Now we know about infrared and other light waves, but they existed always, whether or not we had the scientific ability to see them.

I nodded. I understood.

"Nature doesn't change," she said. "We just don't see sometimes. Or we forget something we already knew."

There were people in South America, she said, long ago, who knew how to make their dreams true.

There were tribes in Africa who had rituals to bring their dreams to life.

"Nature doesn't change," she kept saying. "People do. People forget."

She shined her headlight on a book she brought. Why she didn't show it to me in the daylight, I don't know. Why she waited to tell me all of this on the campout instead of back at our house, also don't know. She didn't usually hide things from me. It was just the two of us. We were best friends.

"I think this is true, Marnie," she said. She shined her headlight on a picture in the book. There were six people, brown skinned, sitting in a circle around a fire. They all had their eyes closed. Above them, coming out of their heads, were these kind of hazy images of those same people, but doing other things.

One wore an elaborate headdress.

"He dreams of being the chief," my mother said.

Another held a baby. Self-explanatory.

One wore a beak on a string tied over his nose, and he had long feathers growing out of his shoulders. The man having that thought sat cross-legged near the fire, but the flying version of him was taking off into the sky.

My mother pulled out another book. I didn't know about any of this. It was like she'd been planning how to tell me. It made me really nervous. I thought we were always honest, but it was like she'd had this secret, and I didn't know for how long.

In the second book there were only three people sitting beside a fire, and there was snow on the ground around them.

Above them, these amazing, beautiful swirls of light. Bright green, purple.

"What is that?" I asked.

"The Aurora Borealis," she said. "The Northern Lights. Those are real. They still exist in northern climates. We could go see them this winter if we wanted."

I didn't know then. I thought we were just talking.

She said that book had the most information out of all of them. It had been written in the 1800s.

"Modern times," she said. That was modern to her. "I think we should go there," she said.

"Where?"

"Alaska." She pointed to the book. "This village where they did it still exists."

Like I said, we didn't have a lot of money. She had to borrow from one of her colleagues. Two tickets from

Utah to Alaska, and then the cost of getting to that village, then their charge for the Northern Lights Experience.

We went over both our winter break. Left a few days after Christmas. We didn't buy each other any gifts. All the money was for the trip.

"We'll spend New Year's under the Northern Lights," my mother said. "It will be unforgettable."

I'd never traveled much, except when we moved or when we went on car trips. I'd never flown on a plane. It was thrilling and scary. But I loved it. I felt like I was four, not sixteen. Everything was so exciting. Even the snack cart.

It was cold, of course. But we'd packed everything warm. We took a second plane, much smaller, a lot scarier, to get closer to the village. Then a van picked us up and took us there.

It was a cute place. Really nice cabins, a nice lodge where you could sit by a fire with fur blankets over you while you drank hot chocolate. I played cards with some other kids who were there with their families. It was fun.

You could just stay there the whole time, or you could pay more to get a snow mobile to take you further out into the wilderness where there were no lights anywhere, just the lights from the sky. They gave you lots of fur blankets, a thermos of hot chocolate or coffee if you wanted, another thermos with soup, some bread and other snacks, and then they'd leave you for a while and come back and pick you up.

We did that. That was my mother's plan all along. To

be left alone out there, under the lights, so she could try her ritual.

She didn't tell me about that. Not ahead of time. I thought we were just there to see the lights.

But once the snowmobiles dropped us off and the people from the lodge said they'd be back in two hours, my mother got us both warm and cozy on our camp chairs and covered in furs, and then she pulled out her book.

Her own book. One she'd been writing, without telling me.

A book filled with rituals about dreams.

Rituals from South America and Africa and Asia, some from Australia.

And ones from tribes in Alaska, involving the Aurora Borealis.

She started with that ritual first. It made the most sense. She spoke words, she made movements, I have to be honest, she scared me.

She wasn't like herself. She was… intense. Intense in a way I had never seen.

She shouted and sang and moved for two hours.

I shivered beneath the furs and watched her.

She started crying after a while. "It doesn't work! Why doesn't it work for me?"

I didn't say anything. I'm not sure she even remembered I was there.

The snowmobiles came back and picked us up. My mother was so depressed.

The next morning she paid for a second night.

"I'll try one of the others," she told me. "Don't give up, Marnie."

I wasn't giving up. I wasn't involved at all. I was like a stuffed animal, just sitting with her while she did it. She didn't talk to me or ask me any questions or ask me for any help.

It was New Year's night. The first night of a new year. My mother sang and hopped around in the snow and waved her arms and shouted words.

I drank cocoa this time because I was cold. And I wanted some comfort. My mother was acting so strange.

But it didn't work. My mother cried again. It was starting to feel like a cycle.

Her excitement, her ideas about how to make it happen this time, then trying, then failing, crying, depressed.

We went out again. And again. We couldn't afford it, but she kept paying.

We had to book extra nights at our cabin too, because she hadn't planned on staying there that long. She thought she would succeed the first night. We had to change our flight back too.

Then finally, January fourth.

The South American chant.

Nothing to do with Aurora Borealis, but it was the right ritual after all.

I won't tell you what it was. You'll try it. I don't want anyone else to ever do it.

The sky. That's how we knew: the sky.

The lights all around us were purple and pink and red. Swirling in giant round waves. So beautiful. So unearthly.

And then my mother said the right words. She moved her arms in just the right way. She sang her song in exactly the right pitch.

The sky became white.

Not swirling anymore, but long fingers reaching down from the heavens, white spears of it, pushing toward the ground, pushing into both of us.

Punching into my chest.

Throwing my mother off her feet into the snow.

It hurt. But it felt glorious. Like something alien entering my body and making me suddenly feel alive. Like I'd been asleep for sixteen years. Now I could see and smell and feel. I could hear everything: the stars, the white light, my mother's heartbeat. The heartbeat of the whole world.

I felt overjoyed. I leapt from my chair onto my feet and started jumping up and down.

My mother was laughing and shouting and crying.

She ran over to me and hugged me. We both jumped up and down together. We were laughing and screaming. I've never felt happier in my life.

"Do something!" my mother shouted. "Come on, Marnie!"

I started running. It felt so natural and wonderful.

Like in a dream.

And like in a dream, the faster I ran, I wanted to go faster still. I ran faster than I ever had in my life.

And it felt natural to stretch out my arms.

And then to move them. Up and down.

And my feet lifted off the snow.

Just like in a dream.

I was dreaming. I'd swear it. Nothing felt the slightest bit real. I soared over my mother's head and could see her gazing up at me, so happy, amazed, happier than I'd ever seen her.

I felt perfect. For a while. Maybe five whole minutes. Then it was like I woke up. Realized this was true.

Panicked.

I started twisting up there in the air. I lost my way. My arms weren't working right anymore. My body felt so heavy and wrong.

I could hear my mother screaming. I was falling so fast toward the snow. She screamed and ran to where I was falling.

But I landed perfectly on my feet.

She stared at me, shocked.

"Marnie."

"Mom." I ran to her and held on to her and both of us cried for a while.

The snowmobiles came back.

We had to act like nothing had happened.

When I hugged her I could feel something different about my mother.

Something warm in the center of her chest.

The next day we paid for the snowmobiles one more time and went out for our final night.

"Try it," my mother said. Even before she did the ritual again.

I felt nervous. Afraid. But also curious and excited.

I ran. Flapped my arms. And lifted off the snow.

My mother tried it. But it didn't work for her.

She tried other things: hopping, running faster, flapping her arms faster—nothing worked.

She was devastated. All that effort, and it had only worked for me.

She did the entire ritual again. Maybe that was the problem. Maybe it only worked for one person at a time.

The lights were green that night, but then they turned white again. The same piercing shards pushing down from the sky.

Into her heart, into mine.

I didn't feel so happy this time.

Just… anxious.

I threw off the fur blankets and started running again. I took off into the sky. I flew like I needed it. Because I did. Flapped hard and then started swimming in the air, my arms pulling me forward like I was swimming against a current.

My mother knelt in the snow and sobbed.

But I had to keep flying. I couldn't come down and console her.

I could see the snowmobiles from the distance and knew I'd have to come back down.

But it made me so angry. I didn't want to have to stop.

But my mother was in bad shape. I knew I needed to help her.

So I flew until the last possible moment, then came down and helped her get under control.

And that was the last time any part of my life felt normal.

We left Alaska. I was a shaking, jittery mess. I couldn't sit still anymore. I couldn't focus on anything. She'd be talking to me and in my head I was saying *shut up, shut up, shut up,* because all I could think about anymore was whether I would ever get to fly again.

It was like someone had infected me with this horrible, insatiable desire. Like those people you read about who scratch their skin off, they can't ever satisfy their itch.

At night I started flying. All night. I'd leave our house as soon as it was dark, and fly for the next twelve hours.

By morning I was exhausted. I couldn't go to school. My mother wasn't speaking to me. She was so distraught that it hadn't worked for her.

And then everything changed again.

One morning I came back from flying and she was up waiting for me in the kitchen.

Ecstatic. So excited.

"I had a dream last night," she said. "One of those falling dreams where you wake up right before you hit the ground."

I waited to hear the rest. I didn't have a good feeling.

"You've had flying dreams since you were a little girl," my mother said. "You always told me."

I could see where this was going. "No, Mom."

"Yes," she said. "We have to try."

She cancelled her classes for the day and we drove to Cedar Breaks.

I begged her not to do it.

It was insane. I begged her not to try.

But she was as jittery as I was, ever since the ritual worked.

I could work out some of that by flying all night long.

She had no place to get rid of the feeling.

There were dark circles under her eyes. She looked exhausted and sick. She kept saying, "Yes, it will work, it worked for you," and I kept telling her no, and then she shouted, "MARNIE! I GET TO HAVE IT TOO!"

And she jumped.

Over the edge of a cliff.

I screamed. I jumped after her, flying, knowing it would be impossible to save her.

I was too weak. I couldn't catch her or carry her. I couldn't carry anything and still flap my arms.

My mother screamed, screamed with joy. As she fell fast down the face of the cliff.

And when she was near the bottom, about to die—

Her body suddenly stopped in midair.

Just like in a dream.

Suspended like she was held up by cables.

Perfectly horizontal, a smooth stop.

I hovered beside her.

My mother laughed.

I laughed too, out of relief.

But it was crazy. I could see that. Much crazier than being able to fly.

"I want to try it again," my mother said.

I didn't argue. I understood what that feeling was like.

Using my arms to keep me up, I pushed her body with my feet. Got her to a place on the side of the cliff where there were places to put her hands and feet so she could climb down the rest of the way.

She was only a few feet from the bottom. It didn't take her long.

We realized there were no trails where we were. It took us the rest of the day to climb out.

I could have flown, easily, but I stayed with my mother. For safety.

Because any time we got high enough out, she would turn around and jump again.

I made her stop falling all the way to the bottom. "We have to get out before dark." So she only fell halfway sometimes, or a quarter, but I couldn't make her stop falling all together.

She'd jump, I'd fly down to her, then push her to the side so she could climb.

It was past dark when we finally made it to the top.

I was worried she'd jump again.

She wasn't thinking clearly anymore. It was like a drug. It took hold.

I held onto her tight and got her into the car. I was afraid to let her drive. I thought she might drive the car off a cliff, so even though I was new to it, I drove.

That night her eyes looked glassy. And she had the biggest smile on her face. She was giddy. Couldn't stop talking. How wonderful it all was, how it felt.

I was exhausted after the day, but I still had needs of my own. I didn't fly as long that night, but I still flew.

And in the morning my mother cancelled her classes again.

This was our life now.

I stopped going to school too. Not because of flying, but to keep my mother safe.

I told people she was home schooling me. She told the university she was sick and needed a leave of absence.

We were almost out of money.

Every day she had to jump.

"Mom, one of us needs to work."

"I know," she said. She tapped her hand against the kitchen table, so much energy she couldn't contain it.

"What are we going to do?" I asked.

"I'll get a loan," she said.

She did, somehow. That bought us another few months.

But by the summer we were behind on our rent and I had to get a job. I started working at a place that served only breakfast and lunch. I didn't make much, but it was something. And I was always free by late afternoon.

My mother and I made a deal. We looked at the maps together and decided the places she could go. We'd been exploring the canyons and knew which ones she could climb out of on her own. She had to fall to a specific spot, but then there were rocks close enough that she could grab and pull herself over to the side.

And I would always fly down there after my shift was over in the afternoon and push her if she was stuck somewhere.

But my mother was a sneak.

No, not my mother, the condition.

Ever since she found out about the ritual, it's like she locked me out.

She lied. More than I realized.

About why we were going to Alaska. About what she was going to do there.

And now, about the jumping.

I came home one afternoon to change into my flying clothes, and there was a note.

Change of plans.

That's all it said.

We had gone over the map the night before. One of her regular routes. No problem.

Change of plans.

My blood froze.

My mother had been acting more and more erratic.

More obsessed.

Taking, I warned her, too many risks.

"But it feels so good," she said with a smile. "The falling. You don't know what it's like."

"I do know, Mom—"

"You don't!" she snapped. "You don't," she said more softly. "I hate always having to climb back up. I just wish I could fall a thousand miles."

Change of plans.

It was like a drug. I knew it. I've felt it in myself. Like something inside your veins. Or invading your brain. Something you can't logic yourself out of.

It doesn't matter if you know it's dangerous. It doesn't

matter if you have a daughter. If you lose your job. If you lose your house.

You need it. You have to have it all the time. Nothing matters but how wonderful it makes you feel.

The car was gone. She always took it. I knew the way to fly to go meet her in the spots where she always went.

She wasn't in any of them.

The car wasn't there.

I flew from canyon to canyon. Cliff after cliff. Already knowing she wasn't there, but I had to look.

When it was dark, I kept looking, calling out for her, screaming.

"MOM! MOTHER! ARE YOU HERE?"

Calling for her until I lost my voice.

So tired of flying I was afraid my arms would give up.

Some time in the early hours I had to rest for a while. It was cold, even in the summer. I wasn't dressed warmly enough. I hunkered in an overhang just to get out of the wind. I slept, badly.

My mother could be suspended somewhere in midair.

No food or water. Cold.

Maybe calling for me, afraid.

In the morning I searched again. I never found her car.

I went home and looked at more maps.

Over the next several days I went to Zion, Escalante, and Bryce. We had talked about camping in those places later in the summer to give her some new places to jump.

I never found her car.

I never found her.

I could see her in my mind's eye, unconscious from

lack of water. Lying horizontal near the bottom of some deep, deep canyon where no one would ever find her.

How long did it take her to realize she'd made a terrible mistake?

That I wouldn't know where to look for her, and couldn't help her over to the side?

When the giddiness had worn off, when she'd fallen further than ever before, when that drug flooded her veins for a while, but then the drug was starting to leave—

Did she call for me?

Not on a phone, there was no signal in the canyons. We had experimented with that before.

Called out for me as a mother for her daughter, "MARNIE! HELP ME!"

Did she call until she was hoarse?

Did she fall asleep that first night still believing I would come and save her?

Or did she fall asleep knowing she would die there and I'd never find her no matter how long I searched?

I did search. For weeks. Knowing she was dead now, but still wanting to find her body.

I stopped working. Let the landlord lock us out. Lock me out. I was alone now. I knew it, but I didn't want to think it.

I turned seventeen in August.

I still searched until the end of September.

I started over. Moved to a new town. Got a new job. Lied about my age. Lied about my name. Lied about everything.

I stopped looking for her. I didn't want to find whatever her body might look like now, picked apart by scavenging animals.

Why had my mother done it? Not the falling—I understand that. It's a compulsion. She couldn't help it. It would be like asking a person not to swallow or blink.

But why did she have to take us to Alaska? Why did she have to do the ritual?

Weren't we happy as we were?

We read books to each other aloud at night, snuggled together on the couch.

We cooked together. We watched movies. We went hiking and camping. I told her everything. I didn't need other friends, I had her.

She didn't need other friends, she had me.

I was smart once. I did well in school. I was the biological daughter of two smart professors. I was going to college. Maybe major in geography. Or anthropology, to follow after my mother.

I did follow after my mother.

But it didn't matter.

I never found her.

3

Tears streamed down Alice's face.

She held her lips tightly together, trying not to cry.

Marnie looked pale and exhausted, almost as white as the pillow behind her.

"It isn't a gift," she said.

"No," Alice said.

"Do you understand why I hate it when they say that?"

Alice nodded. She understood.

She had seen her parents' bodies. Washed of all the blood. Their waxy skin. Looking like mannequins.

It was her decision whether to bury them or burn them. She chose cremation. They were already gone. Not in those bodies anymore. It didn't matter anymore.

"Do you still feel that way?" Alice asked. "That you don't want to find her body?"

Marnie hesitated. Then she shrugged.

Alice pinched her fingers against her eyes. It was too hard. What Marnie had been through was too hard.

"What do you want?" Alice asked her. "For your life now? If you could have anything?"

Marnie turned her face toward the windows, to where a sliver of sunlight managed to sneak into the dark room.

She picked up the green plaid scarf that Alice had given her. She wrapped it around her neck. It felt warm, soft. Cozy. Like someone thought about how to take care of her.

She pulled on the dark blue fleece gloves and then spread her fingers and looked at her hands.

She wasn't sure she could talk. She had said all she could say.

"I don't know," she answered at last. "It's never been an option. It's been… just what it is. All the time, every day."

"Where do you want to live?" Alice asked.

"Someplace warm in the winter, cool in the summer."

"Do you want to work?" Alice asked.

Marnie shook her head. She had worked all her life since she was sixteen. None of it made her feel particularly proud. None of it made her feel like she was doing anything important. It was just to live. Like eating and drinking a few times a day.

"Do you want to…" Alice paused. She looked Marnie in the eyes. "Die?"

"I've thought about it," Marnie said. "But no. I don't. It makes me angry that my mother did. It was a waste. Her whole life was a waste."

Alice didn't know what else to say. What else to ask. It was all so sad and strange.

"Do you feel good when you're doing it?" she asked. "Flying?"

"Yes," Marnie said.

"Then… maybe that's enough," Alice said.

Marnie shrugged. "Maybe." But Alice could see from the troubled look on her thin, drawn face that she wasn't convinced.

She could also see that Marnie was starting to fade. Each blink looked slower and heavier than the one before.

There were still things that Alice needed to discuss. Major Zimholt's offer. Whether Marnie wanted to go. What she wanted to do.

But it could wait a few hours.

Although not much longer than that.

"I'll let you sleep," Alice said quietly, rising from the edge of the bed.

Marnie's gloved hand reached out and gripped Alice by the wrist.

"No," Marnie whispered. "It's not enough."

Alice sank back down beside her. She folded her hand around Marnie's and held it there for a moment. She looked into Marnie's green, bloodshot eyes. There were dark circles beneath them, almost as vivid as the other bruises.

"It's no different from my mother," Marnie said, her voice hoarse. "It's just for me. It's just a drug."

Her grip relaxed.

Alice waited to be sure she was asleep. Then she got up and tucked the sheet and blankets around her.

She picked up the stuffed bear Marnie had given her. She clutched it against her chest and thought about what Marnie said.

It's just for me.

Alice understood that. It wasn't a drug for her, but she knew it was an obsession. Finding out why her parents were dead. Finding every fingerprint on every document and weapon and dollar bill that could be traced to that day when a lone gunman shot into the crowd and killed the people she held most dear.

Did it really matter?

She told herself it did. She told herself she was fighting crime. Finding the bad guys. Helping round them all up so they could never hurt anyone again.

A good reason. Noble.

Lie.

What she wanted was to be able to sleep. To be able to laugh. To wake up and not immediately feel sad. To make it all go away, everything that had happened, reverse time, make the world stop, do the impossible, go back to her life exactly the way it once was.

Just like Marnie wanted.

Alice looked around the room for something she could do. Anything to make Marnie's life easier.

There was no water on the bedside table. She could make sure there was some there when Marnie woke up.

First Alice gathered up all the wrapping paper and took it into the bathroom to throw away.

She stood at Marnie's sink. Looked at her face in the mirror.

That face that always reminded her of her dark-skinned, beautiful mother.

Alice wasn't beautiful, not like that. But her eyes were serious and warm. She knew when Marnie looked at her, she saw a sympathetic face.

You do one thing.

You investigate the bad guys.

You find your parents' killers.

You listen to a woman who wants to tell you her story.

You help her however you can.

Like Major Zimholt. His special suits were genius. Even if he only helped Marnie stay invisible and safe, he had done something.

One thing. Small things. Maybe none of them enough. Not alone, anyway, not just one thing and only that.

You do all of it. All the time. Every day, when the sun comes up.

You are this thing. This person. You are alive. You get to live.

Alice looked for something to write with. The toothpaste would do. She squeezed it onto her finger, then paused, looking at the mirror.

Then she wrote, in large white letters with speckles of whitening power or cavity prevention or whatever the tube promised:

I AM YOUR FRIEND. YOU ARE MY FRIEND.
MERRY CHRISTMAS, MARNIE.

She wiped off her finger on a tissue.

It was enough.

It was a start.

The two of them could figure it out from here.

~

Next in the Dove Season Universe
FINDER

- UFO biologist Dr. Travis Baird investigates a new species of alien in the Arizona desert. Friend or foe? He's about to find out.
- Marnie Stemple has a power that other people want. The only way to stay safe from capture is to keep running. Or is there another way?
- Pilot Sharman Hix fights to communicate with her experimental aircraft before it crashes. How can she get through to it in time?
- Agency analyst Alice Kern continues to search for the answers behind her parents' murder. But is she really ready to hear the truth?
- Scientist-soldier Julie Trident investigates a violent species of alien. What she discovers may change the way humans do battle against them.

Some secrets are meant to stay hidden. Finding the truth can cost you your life.

ABOUT THE AUTHOR

Robin Brande is an award-winning author, former trial attorney, black belt in martial arts, Reiki Master, and wilderness medic. Her outdoor adventures range from the Rocky Mountains to the Alps to Iceland.

She writes in multiple genres, including mystery, adventure, fantasy, science fiction, young adult, romance, and self-help.

For more information:
https://robinbrande.com/

For updates about upcoming installments of DOVE SEASON, along with previews and special discounts, subscribe to the Robin Brande newsletter: https:// robinbrande.com/pages/subscribe.

MORE FROM ROBIN BRANDE

SHOW YOUR BOOK-LOVING STYLE!

AND SCIENCE LOVING, ART LOVING, DOG AND CAT LOVING, AND MORE...

Treat yourself to a soft, comfy, custom-made T-shirt designed by Robin Brande herself, inspired by her own books. You can see all of them at robinbrande.com/collections/t-shirts.

And here's a secret just for you: Use the discount code **READER10** at checkout to get **10% off any items in the store**. That means books, T-shirts, hoodies, mugs—whatever you'd like. Go ahead and treat yourself, book lover.

CERTIFIED
BOOK NERD
CERTIFIED
DOG NERD
CERTIFIED
SCIENCE NERD

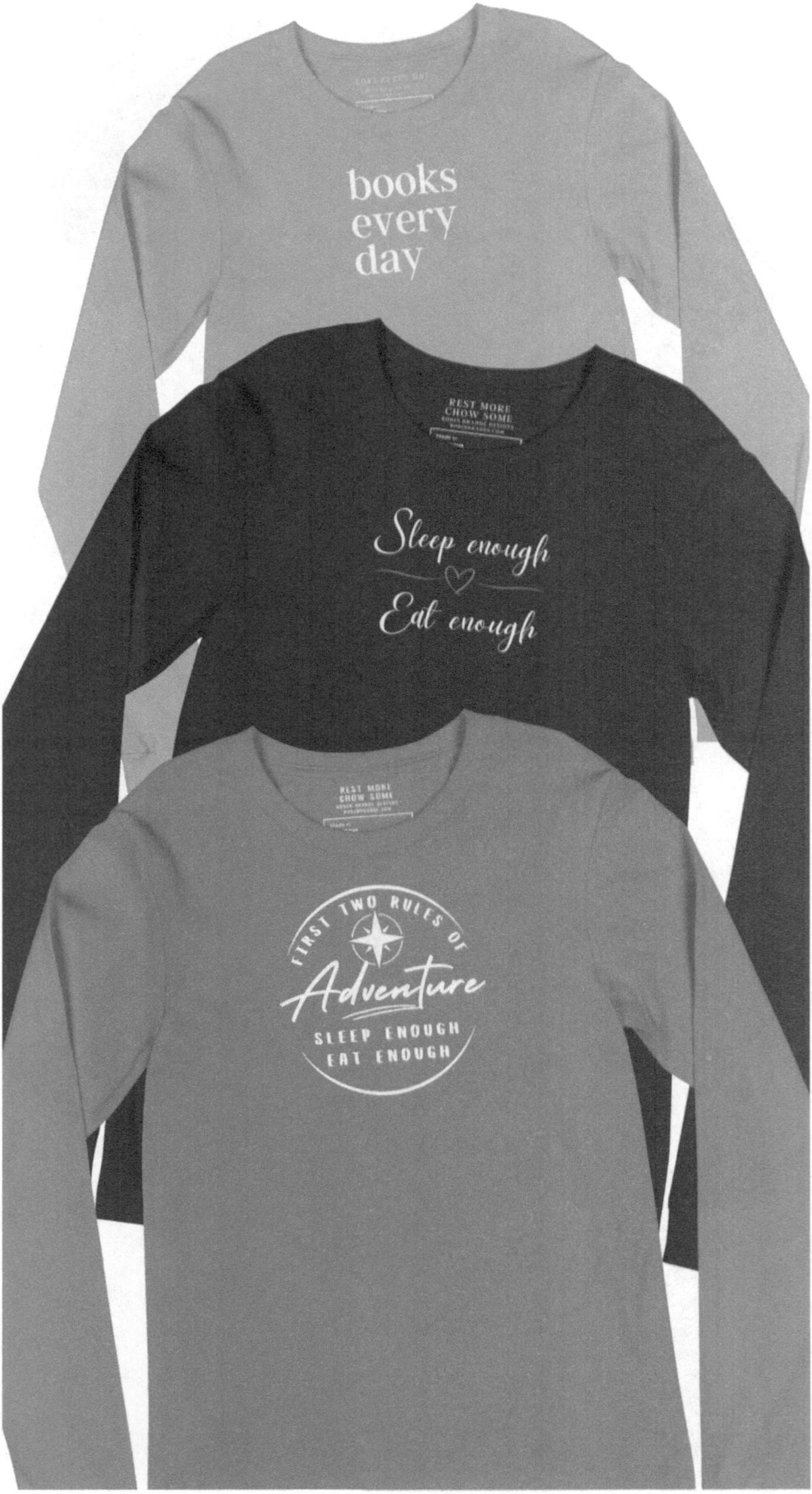

books
every
day
REST MORE
CHOW SOME
Sleep enough
Eat enough
REST MORE
CHOW SOME
FIRST TWO RULES OF
Adventure
SLEEP ENOUGH
EAT ENOUGH

Retired psychology professor Dr. Winifred Parsons spent decades studying the human psyche as a scientist and academic. But she also explored it from another angle: Winnie Parsons is clairvoyant.

Now Winnie uses her psi talent to help clients resolve mysteries that are outside the reach of standard investigations.

The path to justice might be twisted, but Winnie always finds a way.

Life after death, miracle healings, communication with other species...

- *The Water Healers*: A nurse investigates rumors of miracle healers in Mexico.
- *A Drop of Sweat*: A clairvoyant secretly uses her skills to unravel the mystery of who destroyed a scientist's lab.
- *The Refugees*: A volunteer helps the refugees fleeing a planetary disaster.
- *The Bridge*: A grieving widow refuses to believe her husband is gone forever.
- *The Outpost Away from the World*: A scientist returns to the off-the-grid cabin of her childhood and discovers the mysterious secret to her survival.

The mountains can dish it out. But that doesn't mean you have to take it.

- *On Red Mountain*: A woman must survive alone in the mountains after her husband is struck by lightning.
- *The Rescue*: A mountain hermit and his dog race to avert a coming disaster—one that the dog senses before anyone else.
- *Home Deer*: A mountain widow takes matters into her own hands to protect the nearby woodland creatures.
- *The Gold Hunter*: An injured climber's only hope for survival is a stranger who won't give up.
- *Taken at Rustler Pass*: A teen girl fights to survive against the stranger who wants her dead.

High school senior and amateur physicist Audie Masters discovers a parallel universe—along with a parallel version of herself.

It's the adventure of a lifetime.

Now all she has to do is survive it.

Read all four books in the exciting, mind-bending PARALLELO-GRAM QUARTET. You'll never look at the universe or your own life the same way again.